TATTERED HEARTS

MAIL ORDER BRIDES OF SPRING WATER
BOOK ONE

KATHLEEN BALL

I dedicate this book to the people who help me on a daily basis to get my book out for you to read; Bruce Ball, Steve Ball, and Manda Gongora. I also dedicate this book to the most amazing and strong woman I know, Heather Crispin.

And as always this book is for Bruce, Steven, Colt, Clara, Emery and Mavis because I love them.

CHAPTER ONE

Georgie O'Rourke sprinted across the uneven ground, snatched up three-year-old Davey Polk into her arms, and pulled him out of the way of the next wagon in line, saving him from being trampled by the powerful horses' hooves. They fell with a hard thump on the ground, and luckily, Davey landed on top. She looked up, seeking his parents, and discovered the Polk's hadn't even noticed that little Davey was missing.

"Ho! Halt!" yelled one of the guides on horseback. He reined in then jumped down from his black quarter horse and raced toward the pair.

Struggling to comfort a wailing Davey, Georgie was relieved to see Victor headed their way. He was the nicest of the guides, and he never treated her as anything other than a lady.

"Are you hurt?" he asked as he knelt down on one knee next to her. His tan hat shaded his lapis blue eyes, but she figured they would reflect the concern in his voice.

"Can you hold Davey so I can get up?" she asked. She

handed the crying toddler to Victor in relief. Her whole body trembled thinking of what might have happened. It had been a near thing.

The gray-haired, black-eyed wagon master Mr. Wilde galloped to them and scowled when he saw the reason for his train stopping. "Fell out again did he?" He shook his head in disgust. He reached out and took the boy from Victor. "I'll be the one to return this youngster to his parents this time." He rode off with Davey screaming at the top of his lungs.

Victor took off his brown hat and ran his fingers through his wavy dark hair. He replaced his hat and held his hand out to her. She grabbed it and winced as she stood.

"You're hurt."

"I'll be fine I think I scraped my knee is all. We need to press on." Georgie clasped her hands together to try to stop them from shaking. It had been a close one and she thought for sure they'd both be trampled by the horses.

"I'll walk you to your wagon." He escorted her back three wagons and explained to the Wilsons what had happened. They immediately took her inside to check her out.

All the attention embarrassed Georgie. She didn't want to be a bother to the Wilsons. They were kind enough to allow her to travel to Texas with them in exchange for her help with the chores. It was a great deal as far as she was concerned.

Her home state of Tennessee had been ravaged by the Civil War. Her family was gone, and her house had been destroyed. With almost no resources, she had answered an ad in the local paper to become a mail order bride. After the first letter, the gentleman had proposed. She sent off her acceptance and asked him to send any letters to Little Rock. It was the biggest town they'd be going through, and she hoped that letters would reach it.

Happily, she'd received two more letters and was able to write him back. Parker Eastman was his name. He'd been a Confederate officer and now he ran the family ranch. He was a romantic man with the manners of a Southern gentleman. She hadn't recognized his last name but he knew of the O'Rourkes of Tennessee. It was a well-known name that had carried a lot of weight in the now war-torn state.

It was her name that she brought to the marriage. No dowry, few clothes, and no money. She'd been up front about it from the first letter. It didn't matter, he'd written. She was half in love with him already, and she hadn't even met him.

"It doesn't look bad. It's a scrape just like you thought," Mrs. Wilson said. "I'll clean it. I can't imagine being so brave as to jump in front of a wagon like that. The Polks need to come and thank you for what you did for their Davey. My word, they don't look after that child."

Georgie shrugged. "I'm just glad I was there to help. It's hard to believe we're almost at the end of the Southwest Trail. I heard we've actually been in Texas most of the day."

"Have we really?" Mrs. Wilson smiled. "That's great news. I can't wait to meet your intended. I know you're nervous, but from his letters he sounds like a good man. I'm so glad for you. Mr. Wilson and I didn't lose as much as you in the war, and starting over is going to be hard but you'll have a husband to help you."

Georgie's stomach churned. "Yes, I'm fortunate indeed." She hoped beyond hope everything worked out. There was no going back not that there was anything to go back to. "I'm going to walk some more. I get too antsy if I ride too long."

"Be careful."

Georgie nodded as she jumped skillfully from the back of the wagon. Walking was also good for thinking. She usually walked alone. There were other females her age but, they were filled with silly dreams of Texas and how wonderful their lives would be. But they still had parents to shield them from the harshest of realities and they still had a certain innocence about them that she couldn't stand to be around.

Texas was a harsh land, she'd heard. Only the strongest survived, and though she was stronger than most, she knew she wouldn't have things easy. But she'd seen and endured more than she should have already. Now she was both afraid and grateful for the next chapter of her life to start.

They stopped a bit early that day. Mr. Wilde wanted to have a meeting about safety and responsibility. Georgie ended up embarrassed by all the attention paid to her while the Polks actually seemed contrite. Still, they never thanked her. But she hadn't done it for them, so it didn't matter.

As soon as the meeting broke up, she gathered wood for a fire and started making biscuits. It was windy, and she ended up with flour all over her clothing, as well as in her hair and on her face. She'd wait until she was done cooking, though, before she bothered to clean up.

PARKER EASTMAN HAD BEEN WATCHING for the wagon train for more than a week. His patience had run its course by the time he spotted it. Hopefully, this one had his mother's friend Georgia on it. His mother had been so insistent that he be the one to collect her. He had more than enough to do on the ranch but that didn't matter. His mother could be a tyrant at times. Perhaps her friend Georgia O'Rourke of the Tennessee O'Rourkes would soften her disposition.

It had been a tough two years since he'd come home from the war. Swallowing defeat was hard enough, but losing both his brother and father made it almost too much to bear. He had to tamp down his pride almost daily as the Union

Soldiers insulted the people of Texas. They were the victors, and they never let anyone forget it.

He was just grateful he still had a home to come home to. Many of the homes and ranches had been taken over by soldiers. His was too far from town for them to bother with but they sure knew how to get to his place come tax time.

The train stopped, and Parker drove his team toward the group of wagons. He was heartily greeted by the wagon master, a Mr. Wilde.

"Sure is good to be back on Texas soil again," Mr. Wilde said as he shook Parker's hand and then slapped him on the back.

"It's not all roses here either. It's about the same all over the south. I'm looking for a Georgia O'Rourke."

The wagon master smiled and nodded. "Quite a girl you have there. Georgie is always willing to pitch in. She saved a little boy today. Brave she was, running and grabbing him up right before the horses trampled him. They were both lucky. I admire her spirit considering what she's been through. Those Union Soldiers were brutal, and then the Confederates came right behind them and ravaged what was left." He glanced back at the group of wagons. "Well, I didn't mean to talk your ear off. She's right over there at the Wilson wagon."

Parker stared at the woman Mr. Wilde pointed to. Georgie? Certainly she wouldn't have such a nickname.

Why she was nothing but a ragamuffin. Her hair stuck out everywhere, her dress looked to be ready for the ragbag, and she was covered in flour. She glanced up and he was captured by the blueness of her eyes. They were a steel blue and for some reason it made him think she was full of determination. This had to be the wrong woman.

He walked to her as she was bent over the fire and stayed to one side until she stood back up.

"Could you be kind enough to direct me to Miss. O'Rourke?"

A frown drew lines across her forehead. She appeared flustered as she peered at him. She tried to pat down her hair as though seeking to make herself presentable, but she only made it worse. "Who would be asking?"

"I'm Captain Eastman. I've come to collect one Georgia O'Rourke from Tennessee."

He observed as she swallowed hard. "That would be me. It's nice to finally make your acquaintance, Captain."

Trying his best not to look as dismayed as he felt, he tipped his gray hat to her. "My mother speaks very highly of you, Miss."

"Miss? Surely it's proper for us to be on a first name basis?" Her smile was enchanting but it was hard to get past her appearance.

"Are you ready to go? I need to get back to the ranch as soon as I can. I have more work than I can handle."

Her brow furrowed. "We're leaving without getting married first? You insisted on it in your letters. I thought it would be tomorrow." She dusted at her clothing. "I don't usually have flour all over me."

He narrowed his eyes on the little fortune hunter. "I'm sorry, but there is some mistake. I was sent here to collect you on my mother's behalf. There is certainly no marriage involved."

She paled and her hands shook. "But your letters—"

"Madam, I have never written you or any woman a letter. I don't know what game you're playing but I don't intend to participate. Good day." He turned on his heel and strode away. The nerve of some people. *Marriage indeed, that'll be the day.* She'd have to pull off some miracle to be considered marriageable.

"Where are you going?" Mr. Wilde asked. "You promised

your hand in marriage and by golly you're going to keep your word!"

Parker took a step back. "I honestly have no idea what you or Miss O'Rourke are talking about. I wasn't born yesterday. I know most of the scams people are trying to pull. The marriage scam is well known. I work too hard to allow a woman to try to marry me so she can steal my money. You'll have to find someone else. I'm heading back toward Fort Worth. Good day."

"Wait, Mr. Eastman," Wilde called out. "I just recalled I have a letter for you from your mother. I wasn't sure why she sent it to me to keep for you, but maybe I know now." The wagon master hurried to his wagon and came back with a sealed letter addressed to Parker.

The envelope was cool against his palm as he stared at it, and frowned. It was his mother's handwriting, all right. He didn't want to open it; he didn't want to know what she'd cooked up this time. Clenching his jaw, he tore it open anyway, read it, and swore. Lowering the sheet of paper, he stared at Mr. Wilde and then at Miss O'Rourke. This had to be some type of joke. His mother knew he had a strong sense of honor and it seemed that she pledged his hand to Georgia O'Rourke. Ruined his life was what she'd done.

He nodded to Mr. Wilde. "I suppose you're allowed to marry people?"

A grin slid over the wagon master's face and he called out, "Folks, we're having a wedding now!"

Flummoxed, that was the perfect word. Parker was flummoxed, and he was going to kill his meddling mother. He tried to smile, but the best he could do was not frown. Why? Why had she done it? There were plenty of single and widowed women in Texas. It must be the O'Rourke name. Sometimes his mother could be such a snob.

His intended exited her wagon and although she was clean, she still wore rags. He smothered a sigh. Clean rags.

"Got yourself a pretty mail order bride, you did," Mr. Wilde commented.

Parker raised his brow. "Mail order? Are you sure?"

The other man's eyes grew wide. "You didn't know anything about this did you, son? The deed isn't done. You could explain to her… I don't know where'd she go or what she'd do, but it's not your fault."

He momentarily considered leaving, but duty and honor had been drilled into him since he was a boy. He'd marry the urchin. His mother could not have known his intended wore tattered dresses. She'd be good company for his mother, he supposed. He wasn't at the house much anyway.

"Let's get this done so we can leave."

"Georgie! You stand right here. We'll have the Wilsons stand up with you."

Through the whole ceremony, all Parker could think of was all the refined women he'd known. He could hardly look at Georgia. He'd have to grow used to her.

"What? I'm sorry I forgot the ring."

"It's fine," Georgia said.

He expected her to be disappointed, but she wasn't. Most females he knew would have pouted.

At the end of the ceremony, he was supposed to kiss her, but she still had flour on her forehead. He took her hand and kissed the back of it. He was glad of the shy smile she gave him.

"We might as well put your things in my wagon."

"That will be fine. I don't have much." She led him to the Wilsons' wagon and reached in. She pulled out a simple carpetbag and handed it to him.

"Is this all?" He hadn't meant to embarrass her, but by the shade of red her face turned, he had done just that. Another sigh slipped out. "Say your goodbyes. I'll be at the wagon. We need to make tracks while it's still daylight."

Georgie nodded. "I'll be right there."

He felt the heat of her gaze the whole walk to his wagon.

———

TEARS FORMED in her eyes as she tightly hugged the Wilsons. They'd been more than kind to her. Mr. Wilde gave her a fatherly hug, and she started to walk away.

"Wait!" cried a shrill voice.

She turned to find Davey running toward her.

She crouched and gave him a big hug. "You take care now, you hear? I'll miss you something awful." She let go, turned him in the direction of his parents. "Goodbye."

Tears trailed down her face as she walked to her new husband's wagon. He hadn't wanted her. He hadn't proposed to her. He hadn't even known about her. The situation couldn't be worse. She took a deep breath as her confidence plummeted. Circumstances could and had been worse. Whoever Parker was, he'd come through in her time of need. He didn't seem to think much of her, though. That message was clear in his stormy, whiskey brown eyes.

He held out his hand and helped her onto the wagon. She settled on the hard bench as he climbed up on his side. Soon they were off. She wanted to say something, but she didn't know what to say. Everything she thought she knew was a lie. How could his mother have done such a thing?

THEY HEADED down a heavily rutted trail, then Parker turned onto a trail that looked little used.

"How far is your ranch? You do have a ranch, don't you?" She held her breath hoping he said yes.

He turned his head and looked at her. "Yes I do own a ranch. It's a cattle ranch, and it takes most of my time. It's over a week away." He turned back and watched the trail.

"You've been away from it two weeks already?"

He gave a silent nod.

"I'm sorry it never occurred to me that I'd take up so many weeks of your time. Maybe I could have found a wagon going your way. I should have tried."

Some of the tension seemed to leave his body as his shoulders relaxed. "You didn't know. You were as duped as I was. My mother is meddlesome, I'm afraid. I'm all she has left. We lost my father and brother to the war effort, and she didn't understand why her *maids* left her. She thought of them as family, she said." He shrugged. "You don't own family, of course, but she grew up on a plantation with slaves. She insisted they all accompany us to Texas. My father was the same way except he never lived to see them emancipated."

Georgie mulled over his words, unsure how to respond.

"My brother and I both swore we'd never own another human," Parker continued. "I'm capable of doing any of the work required, and now I have plenty of men who work for me. I wanted to hire some black women to help take care of the house, but I didn't dare. My mother would have expected them to bow to her." He glanced at Georgie. "I'm sorry. I don't even know how you feel about slavery, or if you grew up with them. Everyone seems to have their own distinct opinion on the subject. It's led to a lot of discord in my area of Texas."

She squirmed a bit, trying to figure out what to say. "I grew up on a fine plantation, and yes we owned slaves. I owned Betsy. I never gave a thought to it being wrong. It was just how things were. I hated the treatment the overseer meted out. But I was just a female. I was expected to smile and know how to arrange flowers." She shook her head. "Things are so different now."

"Yes, things are different." He pulled off the trail and stopped. "We might as well make camp."

She jumped down without his help. She was frightened of what came after the sun went down. Betsy had told her horror stories about what happened between men and women. "I'll gather some wood," she called as she went into the woods. A moment alone was what she needed.

She stopped and leaned back against a big tree trunk. What if he didn't like her? She'd never had a beau. The war started just before her sixteenth birthday. There were older men willing but her father put a firm stop to their attempts at courting. Maybe she wasn't likable. No one had ever told her she'd be the belle of the ball someday. Not like they'd told… She shivered. It hurt too much to think about. She needed to keep busy. Pushing away from the tree, she found and carried a big pile of wood.

Was there something wrong with Parker? Why not find a wife closer to home? She expected Union soldiers to lie. She expected carpetbaggers to lie. She did not expect a Southern mother of a captain of the Confederate Army to lie. She cleared the heaviest part of the woods and pasted a smile on her face.

Well, she was married, and she had no choices left. She dropped the armful of wood and then stacked it by the fire pit that Parker had made. Where was he? A twig snapped behind her, and she quickly turned around, but she didn't see anyone or anything, and a shudder rippled through her. Who knew what animals were in the woods?

Glancing at the horses, she relaxed. They were calmly grazing on the grass. They would have alerted her to trouble. She went to the back of the wagon and put the back down before she climbed in. She could start getting the evening meal prepared. There wasn't much in this wagon compared to the wagons in the wagon train. Those wagons had been filled with everything the owners had.

She quickly found the flour and almost laughed. He'd seen her at her worst, yet he'd still married her. Why? He could have ridden away. She might have if the shoe was on the other foot.

"Georgia?" He had a nice deep voice.

"I'm in the wagon." She grabbed what she needed to make biscuits and climbed back out. Parker was getting the fire going. When she approached him, she made sure her face was graced by a smile. His mouth curved upward as well. Her lips twitched.

"I just set a couple snares. There are rabbit trails everywhere, it seems." He put more wood on the fire as soon as he had a flame.

"That must be what I heard."

He quickly glanced up at her. "What kind of noise was it?"

"I heard a twig snap. I looked, but I didn't see anything. The horses didn't react so I didn't worry."

He studied her for a moment. "That is a good indicator. I have to say I'm surprised you'd know that."

This time her smile was real. "A girl learns a lot when she only has herself to depend on."

He frowned but didn't ask her to elaborate. He probably didn't want to know. Everyone had a hard luck story about the war. Both sides had suffered.

"I'll just get the biscuits ready to put in the Dutch oven."

He smiled. "That will go good with the leftover stew from last night. Rabbits have been plentiful In this part of the trip. I'm sure I'll be able to get a deer in a few days. I'm glad you can cook. I expected a woman from the south to be pampered."

She gave him a sad smile. "Once upon a time I was

pampered. But you learn what you have to, and you survive the best you can. I saw women wither and take any proposal even from sharecroppers. Not that marrying a sharecropper is bad, but those women were humiliated and wouldn't meet my eye when our paths crossed."

"Where did you live?"

"I converted the cookhouse to my living area. It was the only building that didn't burn. The slave quarters were still intact but I didn't want to disturb them. I was no longer their responsibility even though many checked on me and tried to help. They didn't know where to go and many stayed. They had a large garden of their own that hadn't been pillaged. I helped many find their family members that they'd been separated from and brought them back to my property. In the end, we worked together to keep everyone fed." Sorrow overtook her and she shook her head. "I cautioned them to make a plan since I could not pay the taxes. It was very likely we'd be run off the land."

She finished with the biscuits. "It was pure luck I saw the ad you – I mean your mother placed in the paper. I didn't know what to do. I was thinking about going north but I didn't know if I'd be welcome up there. I divided my mother's jewelry between me and Betsy. I knew we'd get cheated if we tried to sell it in Tennessee, but I figured it would be useful for something. It got me to St. Louis where I was able to join a wagon train heading this way."

"Why didn't you use it to pay the taxes?" he asked.

"The price was the jewelry plus my virtue. What would happen next year? It didn't make good business sense."

"It's been rough for you." His voice was gentle and sincere. She'd heard it all before but no one ever really meant it.

"It was hard for most. But here I am, married to a man who didn't know he was supposed to be my groom. That must gall you. I bet having been a captain you're used to making your own decisions."

An ironic smile twisted Parker's lips. "You'll soon learn that my mother is the general in the family." He chuckled.

"Was there someone back home you had your eye on? Did you have an understanding with any woman?" She held her breath.

He shook his head. "I'm always too busy to socialize. So the answer is no. I have no interest in any woman."

Including her. Georgie put the stew on to heat. She knew what it felt like to have choices taken away. "I'm sorry you got stuck with me. The letters were so beautiful, and I thought I knew you through them, but I really don't know you at all, do I?"

"I'm afraid you'll find that I don't have a romantic bone in my body. I am the oldest son, the responsible one, the one who was to take over the ranch someday, so I didn't get much free time to think about much other than cattle. Then the war broke out." He shrugged his left shoulder. "It'll be all right. The house is big, not a plantation, mind you, but it's nice. It's heavily guarded against the soldiers, carpetbaggers, outlaws, and Indians."

"Oh my, are we safe traveling alone?" She peered around into the woods.

"We'll be fine."

If those few words were meant to comfort her, they didn't. "How many guns do you have?"

"You shoot?" His voice was full of doubt.

"Of course I do. That's how I'm still alive. I'm a good shot too." She stirred the stew and checked the biscuits. "It's almost ready."

"Have you ever shot a man?"

Her eyes grew wide as her heart took up a frantic

pounding against her ribs. She didn't like to think about it. "I only shot people who deserved it."

He cocked his right brow but he didn't ask anything more. "I'll grab a couple plates."

She sighed in relief as her heartbeat went back to normal. So much had happened and she tried to put it all out of her mind.

CHAPTER TWO

Thunder clapped and rumbled, and it was coming closer. Parker hoped that Georgia wouldn't be too opposed to him climbing into the wagon with her. The anticipated rain came pouring down, a sudden cloudburst that soaked everything around them in moments. He grabbed his blankets and his rifle from under the wagon and scrambled for the inside of the wagon.

To his surprise, she was waiting at the back and dragged his blankets in for him. He handed her the rifle and climbed in.

"Sorry about this."

She wrapped one of her blankets around her thin nightgown. "It's not a problem. There's plenty of room."

"Some women would have objected," he replied as he turned the oil lamp brighter. Her blond hair hung in loose curls down her back. It was lovely and reminded him of silk. What would it feel like to touch it? Her face turned rosy under his regard. "I've embarrassed you."

"No, well yes. I'm not used to anyone looking at me as though I'm actually attractive. I'm used to speculative leers from most men. The kind that are only because I'm female, not because I looked a certain way. I know I'm plain and it's fine."

He was about to object but decided it would only embarrass her more. "It's been awkward between us since after we ate. I know you were nervous that I'd plan to bed you."

She averted her gaze to the wagon floor, her cheeks flushing a deeper shade of red.

"I've done it again. What I'm trying to say is, that can wait until we know each other. Don't get me wrong, it will happen. I want children and I… well I won't need to go into town to the saloon anymore." He laughed. "Every time I open my mouth I make things worse. I don't mean to disturb your delicate sensibilities. I'm not as gentlemanly as I was before the war. Forgive me?"

She chewed on her lower lip then allowed a gentle smile. "I respect your candor. Yes, I blush easily. I've never— I've had to fight off men to keep myself pure for my husband. I'm not ignorant as to what goes on between a man and his wife. Waiting is more than fine with me. To be honest I wish it never had to happen. It's not you, it's with any man. I've seen the brutality, and I've heard the screams."

He laid out his blankets next to hers. "It's supposed to be pleasurable."

She gave him a look of disbelief before she glanced away. "I'm rather tired."

"Of course, get into bed and I'll turn out the lamp."

She gave him a quick glance and then burrowed under her blankets, lying as far away from his bedroll as she could.

His lips twitched in amusement. She acted like a tough pioneer woman one minute and like a nun the next. She was a puzzle, his wife. Wife… How the heck had that happened? He had a lot to discuss with his mother. This time she'd gone too far. At least Georgia had a kind heart. He'd gotten lucky.

He awoke to moaning and thrashing and for a moment, he didn't know where he was. He sat up and realized Georgia was having a bad dream. She cried out and tears streamed down her face. He put his arms around her, and she slugged him in the eye. He winced at the powerful hit.

"Georgia, wake up! It's a dream."

It took a minute but she finally stirred and woke with a groan. "What are you doing?" she asked as she pushed at his chest.

He rubbed his hands up and down her arms. "You were crying out in your sleep."

She relaxed and her body sagged back onto the bed. "I'm sorry I woke you. I have dreams sometimes, I guess."

"As long as you're all right."

"Yes. We should get some sleep."

"Georgia?"

"Yes?"

"Do you have these dreams a lot?"

It took her a while before she answered. "Yes, I keep hoping they'll stop. If they don't, I'll forever be waking you up." Her voice sounded as though she'd somehow failed him.

"It's the war. We all have our demons. I have bad dreams at times too. Sometimes I think it took a lot of my compassion for others away. Bitterness seems to come easy at times, and I was never like that before. I think we've lived through impossible situations and seen some terrible things. I'm not sure if it will ever go away, but I am glad we'll understand each other since we both suffered."

She gave him a quick nod. "It will be easier to be married to you rather than someone who would think the devil lived in me. I hoped that the dreams would just fade once I was married and you'd never know."

He lay on his back and put his arm around her slender shoulder. Gently, he drew her nearer until her head rested on his shoulder. Surprise raced through him as she moved her whole body closer to him. Perhaps they'd be able to offer each other a bit of comfort. He couldn't talk about the war with his mother, and his men all bragged about how many men they'd killed. He'd felt isolated with his thoughts. But now… he felt more relaxed than he had in a very long time. Maybe having Georgia around would be a good thing.

IT STILL POURED when Georgie woke. As soon as her eyes opened, she realized she was lying with her head on Parker's chest. She slowly moved her head and then she felt the rumbling under her ear. He was laughing.

She sat up and stared at him. "What's so funny?"

"You, trying to move away from me so I wouldn't notice. I've been awake for a little bit." The merriment in his eyes riveted her to him.

"I haven't heard much laughter in the last year. It sounds good." She smiled at him and glanced around the wagon. "Do you think the rain will continue?"

"Probably, but we need to keep moving. I'd hate to get stuck in all this mud. As it is, I'll have to push while the horses pull. You can stay inside and stay dry."

She shook her head as she reached for her clothes. "I can pull the horses as you push. There are extra biscuits from last night and day-old coffee. It'll be cold, but I think we'll manage until it stops raining. I put wood inside last night in case of rain."

He gazed at her for a moment and then nodded. "I didn't even think about dry wood."

"Doing without makes you remember the little things that need to be done. Others on the wagon train didn't heed the wagon master's advice, and they had to go without. The

Wilsons, though lovely people, didn't believe in sharing what was theirs."

Parker reached out and took her hand. "You would have shared."

His hand was so big and strong and for a moment, she wanted to weep. Here was someone who she could lean on for a bit. It felt as though she'd been fighting a losing battle alone for so very long.

"Could you turn your back while I dress?"

"Of course. I'll dress at the same time." His grin matched the twinkle in his eyes. "No peeking please."

This time she laughed, and it sounded so very strange to her. "I'll try to control myself." She put her hand over her mouth. This wasn't the type of banter one partook in with a man she hardly knew. "I apologize, that wasn't very ladylike."

From behind her came the rustling of clothing. "I rather enjoyed it. You are a pleasant surprise. I thought you were one of my mother's friends. Her friends had all been part of the elite circles. It's been a while since she was the matron of Charleston. She misses it all. The balls, the gossip, the power to ruin a person's reputation with a rumor whispered to the right people. I like the ranch better. Every mother in Charleston eyed me as a potential husband for their daughters. I wasn't looking for a wife. I was too young to tie myself down."

She pulled up her hose and put on her shoes. "You were lucky to slip out of their clutches. Mothers on a marriage mission could be ruthless. My sister, Amy, was the belle of the ball right before the war broke out, and she had all sorts of offers."

"Did she marry?"

"She thought the war would be quick and she'd have plenty of time to be courted by all the suitors. She bemoaned her bad decision night and day."

"I'm sorry to hear that. Where is she now?"

"I buried her behind the burned-out house." Tears filled her eyes and she angrily brushed them away. "I'm ready."

"I have an extra rain slicker. Let's get it on you." He held up the large garment and then smiled. "We'll roll up the sleeves."

She put it on and stood still while Parker rolled the sleeves several times. He pulled out a cowboy hat and placed it on her. It engulfed her head. Grimacing, he reached to take it off.

"Leave it. I can see and that's all that counts. Make do is what I like to say."

He nodded, put on his gear, and climbed out the back. She followed him to the rear of the wagon and waited until he helped her down. Goodness he was a strong one. Most of the Confederate Soldiers she'd last seen were so thin and weak. If only they'd all had ranches to return to. In Tennessee, so many came back to burned-down homes and missing family members. Many had stopped at her place and asked if she'd seen their loved ones. Most were dead, and it was so excruciatingly hard to have to tell the returning soldiers what had happened.

She helped him harness the horses, and they both studied the wagon wheels. They weren't as bogged down as she'd have thought they'd be. Next, she went to the front and grabbed the lines. She pulled when he called for her to do so, and she almost fell when they came forward so fast they surprised her. She led them up to higher ground and waited for Parker.

Parker took the lines and tied them around the brakes. "Come let's get you out of the rain." He took her hand and led her to the back and then lifted her inside.

"Only for a little while. I can spell you at driving the wagon. I had to drive my share with the Wilsons."

He looked as though he was going to refuse her help but in the next moment, he nodded. "That would be a big help." He started to walk away, then turned and looked over his shoulder. "I'm going to check my snares, and then we'll get moving."

Quickly she took off her rain slicker and muddy boots. Next, she poured a cup of cold coffee and put preserves on a few biscuits. She made her way to the front of the wagon, pleased to see he had returned with some game and taken his seat. She waited for him to urge the horses forward and then handed him the coffee first. "Drink this then I'll hand you the biscuits."

He smiled his thanks as he drove on, drinking his coffee and then eating his biscuits.

HE ONLY DROVE for a few hours when the rain stopped and then a few more until he came upon dry land. He pulled the horses to a halt. They needed to warm up and dry out. He automatically lifted Georgia out of the wagon and built a fire. He headed to a nearby stream and hauled back some water.

She had the coffee ready to go and as soon as he brought her the water, she poured it into the coffee pot and set it on the fire.

He grabbed the three rabbits he'd pulled out of his snares before they left. "I'll dress these and maybe we can have a hot meal. I'm not sure if we'll get a soaking rain again today. The clouds are dark, but they just may blow over us."

"I'll get the stew ready for the meat. It'll be the easiest to reheat tonight. And I can make corn bread."

His eyebrows rose. "Corn bread? I wish I had you on the trip out there. I ate an amazing amount of beans."

She turned a pretty shade of pink. "I was always in the kitchen bothering everyone, trying to learn how to cook. When my mother found out, she forbade me to go in there but I still did. I had to be very careful. She'd have taken her displeasure out on the women working in the kitchen if I was caught again. One day she did find me and what she did to one of the workers was so disturbing, I never went into the kitchen again. I couldn't even look at the servers."

"I've seen enough of that type of thing to last me a lifetime too. Things are changing but not fast enough. My mother is a prime example of someone who refuses to put the past away. I'll apologize in advance. I have no idea what the house will look like when we return. No one wants to work for her. She thinks nothing of lashing out at someone and hurting them. I have taken her crops away and burned them, but she always gets another."

Georgie put her hand over her mouth. "Oh my, I though you meant that she lashed out with her tongue. She's sounds a bit dangerous."

"Georgia, she'll be happy to see you."

"I'd much rather you called me Georgie. I prefer it."

He stared at her for a moment, taken off guard. "Georgie"

"Yes, it's what my father and sister called me. Georgia seemed too formal, I suppose."

"I'll try to remember to call you Georgie."

"That's all I can ask. Now let me finish the meal and we'll be eating in no time."

He grabbed the wet slickers and hats from inside the wagon and laid them out to dry in the warm sun. It had been nice having her in his arms last night, but he probably wouldn't have another excuse come evening.

She stared intently at him while he took his first bite. Luckily, he was able to smile and did not have to pretend. "You have a gift for cooking. I haven't had anything this good

24

in a very long while. You can cook for me anytime." Then he quickly shook his head. "I'm sorry. I didn't mean to infer you'd have to cook once we got home."

"Why not?"

"Surely you'll want to do whatever it is that fine ladies do all day."

She laughed, and he liked the melodious sound of it. "Seat myself on an uncomfortable chair that makes me sit up straight and tall all day pretending to enjoy doing needle work? Then of course, there is the afternoon tea to look forward to. I'll assume your mother would consider it her honor to pour. Then I go and change my clothes and wait for you to come home. You'll change your clothes and escort us to dinner where we talk about nothing really. Your work wouldn't be appropriate, since you use your hands to do it. Then after dinner, you can escape while I spend more time with your mother. I'll say I want to take a walk and she'll say no. I'll retire for the evening wondering if you'll come to bed or not."

She looked out at the horizon for a bit and then gazed at him. "I'd much rather have something to do. If cooking will be of help, I'd gladly do it. I don't want to live by the strictures of society." Her eyes filled with worry.

"There isn't much society where we are, though mother insists we act what she refers to as 'civilized.' Don't worry, you'll find something you'll be happy to do. I don't expect you to sit all day. Do you ride?"

"My father had fine stables at one time," she answered proudly.

"Side saddle?"

"Well, of course."

"I'll teach you how to ride astride. The land is so uneven it's dangerous using a sidesaddle."

Her face grew bright red, but she gave a resolute nod. "I'm game."

He wasn't positive if she really was. "We have different riding clothes in Texas. It's a split skirt for women to wear while riding. And with leather boots, you won't have your ankles showing."

She sighed in relief. "I'm looking forward to it."

"I'll help you clean up so we can get going. I have been gone from my ranch a long time it seems. Anything could've happened."

She gathered the plates. "Like what?"

"Men stealing my land, my cattle, and the union soldiers can be spiteful. And of course there are the outlaws and the Comanche. I trust my men except if someone tried to claim that the land was originally theirs they wouldn't be able to take care of it. There have been many such claims made, but I was there before the war. That land is mine, and I plan to keep it for us."

"Sounds like a dangerous place. What about renegade bands of Confederate Soldiers? They've caused a lot of destruction in Tennessee. I'm trying to understand it all, but nothing about the war ever made sense to me. We lost so much. Too much that we can never get back." She turned away from him but he saw the slight shaking of her shoulders.

Parker put the pot he carried onto the wagon's back gate. He then walked toward Georgie and gently laid his hands on her shoulders. When he turned her around, his heart hurt for her many tears, and he pulled her close, hoping to offer some sort of comfort. A hug could never make up for everything she'd been through, but sometimes it was nice to know that someone understood and cared. He stroked her back as his shirt became damp from tears.

She slowly relaxed but she held on to him. When she

finally let go she gave him a sheepish look and went about cleaning up. She was one strong woman, and he found himself admiring her.

He'd ridden up to many charred and burned out houses with his men, and the destruction he had seen was both devastating and uncalled for. There were usually a few dead, mutilated bodies lying about, and the sheer grief the survivors displayed was unimaginable. They had never had the time to stay and offer comfort. They hadn't had food or any other supplies to give them. He had always felt like a failure as he rode away.

HE MUST THINK HER A NINNY. She was always crying. She'd had to be the strong one for so long that it was nice to have someone comfort her for a change. As each disaster befell her family and friends, she had been the one they'd turned to. She had grown tired of saying that everything would work out somehow. Even when she didn't believe it to be true. She'd planned to go north as soon as the house burned but she had been needed. It was just as well or she would never have seen the ad to marry Parker.

She sat on the wagon bench watching the scenery of massive trees go by. "Are you sure you don't have a woman waiting for you at your home? You didn't know about me, and a man like you must have plenty of women wanting you for a husband."

He glanced away and she could see the back of his neck turn red. He looked forward and was silent for a bit. "I suppose there are women interested, but I am not. My mother was always inviting people to the house for dinner. She'd get all her fancy dinnerware out and act better than her guests. I was surprised by the amount of people who fed into her act. But like I said, I didn't have time. I was always working. Though I suppose if someone had really caught my eye I could have made time for her. Many were the same age as you but not mature in any manner. They were still pampered girls despite the war."

"If they still had dresses to wear to a dinner then I don't think they knew the war as intimately as some of us did," Georgie suggested. "I bet they aren't afraid to close their eyes at night or see the back of someone in a crowd and think it's their father or brother. I've been known to run after men a time or two. Hope filled me as I ran but the disappointment when I realized they weren't either of the men I sought was almost too much to bear. I'm hoping we can have a fresh start together." She bit her bottom lip. Maybe she was being too forward.

Parker leaned a bit and bumped his shoulder to hers and grinned. "I'd like that."

For the rest of the day his words repeated in her head. It filled her with optimism.

He found another fine spot for them to stop that night. There were plenty of trees for privacy and a stream close by.

Once again, she went to gather wood, but she stopped in her tracks when she saw a blur of gray moving ahead of her. She walked as silently as she could until she was well hidden behind a tree. If there was one there was bound to be more, many more. Her limbs trembled as she hid but she needed to warn Parker. Taking a deep breath, she started toward camp.

Without warning, she was grabbed from behind and a filthy hand covered her mouth. The man pushed her to walk ahead of him. It was apparent he knew where they were camped. She kicked his shin with her heel, but all that accomplished was the man pulling a knife and holding it to her throat. Burning pain began in her neck and her breath caught. He'd nicked her. From the trickling wet sensation, she knew she was bleeding.

She walked into sight of the wagon and was relieved that Parker wasn't there.

"Where's your man?" The soldier pushed her and she stumbled, forward.

She landed hard on her side and winced as she studied her captor. The soldier wasn't as dirty as his hands were. His hair looked washed, and his uniform wasn't stained or frayed. "My husband died. I'm all alone." She lifted her chin and stared him down. "Where's the rest of your merry band of men?"

His brows furrowed. "My what?"

She shook her head. "Where are the rest of the men you're with?"

"Probably watching me. They'd probably prefer it if you took your clothes off." His grin sickened her.

"They'll be disappointed. I have no plans to disrobe for anyone." She gave him her best glare.

"You're Southern."

"Of course I am. I haven't come across too many Northern women lately."

"Unfortunately, I have. They've been coming with their husbands to steal our land. Heck, what am I supposed to do with you now?"

"Excuse me? Do with me?"

"Well I can't very well take advantage of one of our own. It wouldn't be right. You shouldn't be traveling alone. There are too many who'd use you and kill ya. Do you have any food?" He walked to the wagon and looked inside. "Come on in boys, there's food!"

She watched as five more soldiers emerged from the forest. They were polite enough except for one who had his eyes full of lust. He smiled, revealing his bottom teeth were black.

"Taggart, leave her be."

"Maxwell, I don't have to do what you say. The war is over."

"Taggart, if you look at my wife like that again, I'll put a bullet in your skull."

Georgie's jaw dropped. Parker knew these men? She closed her eyes as she sagged back against a wagon wheel.

"Sorry, Captain. I didn't know yous was married."

"I'm a newlywed. This is my wife Georgie O'Rourke Eastman from the great state of Tennessee." Parker knelt at her side and put his arms around her. "Are you all right?"

"I am now that you're here. I need a pistol of my own to carry."

"Yes, you do. Maxwell, grab a crate out of the back for my wife, will ya?" Parker helped her to stand then led her to the crate and seated her. "So, what's the meaning of you scaring my bride?"

"We didn't know she was a Southern lady, Captain," a short man said.

"Hard to tell by looking isn't it, Stookey?" Parker asked.

"Yes sir. She isn't finely dressed. It wasn't until we heard her accent that we realized…"

"You men looking for work? Honest work?"

"What did you have in mind, Captain?" Maxwell asked.

"I need guards at my ranch. But for now, I'd like a few of you to escort us there and the rest of you to get there as quickly as you can. My foreman is William Cabot. He'll get you clothed in other garments. I don't want you used for target practice. Tell him to introduce you to my mother so she doesn't shoot you either." His lips twitched as the men's eyes widened at the last part. "I'll write a letter of introduction for you. Wait here a second." He turned and caught Georgie's gaze. "I'd like to talk to you if that's all right?"

She nodded and took his offered hand. It felt reassuring as he lifted her up into the wagon. As soon as he climbed in behind her, he pulled her into his arms and kissed her soundly. Her body felt warm all over and as the kiss deepened, it seemed to have a hint of urgency to it. He pulled her close and kissed her temple.

"It startled me when I saw you surrounded by soldiers until I realized that they once served under me. I never should have let you go off on your own, and yes, I'll give you a pistol. My heart was beating so fast I thought it would explode. But all is well now." He took a step back and lifted her chin until their eyes met. "They didn't hurt you, did they?"

"No, I was frightened for a bit, but I planned to fight them if they tried to touch me. The whole time I kept thinking I would no longer be pure for my husband. I wouldn't have won if I fought them, but I hoped it would buy me some time until you got back." She shook her head. "And at the same time, I didn't want you walking into the whole mess."

He grabbed a cloth and wiped the blood from her neck. "You're still shaking."

"I probably will be for a while," she admitted. "But you don't need to worry about me. I'm going to be just fine. Write your letter and then let some of them be on their way." She gave him a small smile.

He leaned down again and kissed her nice and slow. This time he put his tongue in her mouth, surprising her. People really kissed that way? It was actually nice, she decided after her initial shock wore off. He lifted his head and smiled into her eyes.

Climbing back out of the wagon, she tried not to smile but

she couldn't help it. He made her feel special, and she couldn't remember a time when she'd been made to feel that way. She noticed that the firewood had been gathered and water had been hauled. She'd make hoe cakes as soon as Parker was done. She'd need to get back into the wagon to grab all the ingredients.

PARKER WATCHED as the ever-changing colors of the firelight played upon Georgie's face and hair. She was radiant, and he couldn't keep his gaze from her. He'd relived their kiss in his mind many times that evening. It had been the best kiss he'd ever experienced, and he was trying to puzzle out why.

When he held her close, she seemed to fit perfectly with him. It hadn't been a chore to hold her; it was an exciting pleasure. He'd felt young and unjaded for a time. A smile spread across his face. She wasn't schooled in the art of kissing, and it thrilled him to know he was the one teaching her. The sweet sounds she made when he deepened the kiss had him feeling ten feet tall. Then she kissed him back with passion, real passion. He'd kissed plenty of women but most of them pretended their eagerness. Then again, he'd also paid those women.

His wife was certainly a surprise in more ways than one. Besides him not knowing he was to be married, Georgia was so unlike any other woman he'd come across. She had grit and courage. She'd seen the worst, and she still had hope for the future. He'd gotten lucky considering his mother had picked her because of her pedigree.

His smile grew wider.

"What's so funny?" she whispered after she made her way around the fire and sat next to him.

"I was thinking my mother probably thought she ordered a proper Southern lady for me."

Frowning, she crossed her arms in front of her. "I'm not a proper lady? I do try my best, you know but it isn't always easy. I do try to be gracious and have good manners." With a restless hand, she smoothed a hand over her ragged skirt. "I don't have the clothes to look the part." She stared into the fire.

He stood and offered her his hand. He'd insulted her. "Let's go to bed and let the men rest."

Georgie stood. "Good night, gentlemen." She gave them a slight regal nod and walked to the wagon with her small hand in his. She didn't wait for him to lift her into the wagon but scurried into it on her own.

Parker sighed. He had some quick explaining to do. She had her back to him pulling her nightgown on when he climbed in. She didn't say a word, but she didn't glare at him either.

"Good night." She lay down with her back to him.

He took his shirt off and lay right behind her, putting his arm around her waist. He then pulled her close so their bodies were touching. "I'm sorry."

She remained silent.

He kissed her neck. "Let me explain what I meant out there. You're not a pampered girl who needs constant instruction. You've been more of a partner to me than I ever expected a woman to be. I was brought up same as you, where the man made all decisions and the wife just smiled. I don't want a wife like that. I want you. You have a good head on your shoulders, and you are just what is needed to help rebuild Texas. I didn't mean you weren't proper. I'm glad I wasn't sitting around the fire with someone with hoop skirts and white gloves on. I'm proud of the woman you are and I'm proud you're mine."

She pushed back against him, getting closer. "Thank you for explaining. I was never very good at the whole pampered thing. My mother often bemoaned that no man would ever want me. My sister Amy was beautiful, and I didn't come close to her perfection. Even my father preferred to gaze upon her, and all he gave me were disapproving glares. I tried. I tried harder than anyone could have tried to be beautiful and graceful and simpering. I spent hours in front of the mirror, but all I saw reflected back was a failure. I never got new dresses. I wore hand-me-downs from Amy. We had more than enough money for me to have new dresses, but it was meant as a slight to me."

"You're not a failure at anything as far as I can see," he whispered into her ear. She trembled so hard he could feel it.

"Being close to you makes me feel strange inside. I've never felt this way before," she confessed.

"We share an attraction for one another."

She pushed back against him again and he gritted his teeth. She had no idea that she shouldn't rub certain areas of him.

"We need to get some sleep," he said when he could speak. "Tomorrow I want to be able to go as long as the horses are willing." He pulled away a bit but kept his arms around her waist.

"Good night. I'll help however I can."

She would and then some. He felt bad for how her parents had treated her. Apparently she had always been second best, if that. He knew his brother Monty had often felt the same way. Parker had told Monty it didn't matter, but in the end, Monty had felt pushed to join one of the first Texas regiments and he'd been killed in their first battle. That was still hard to deal with.

CHAPTER THREE

*G*eorgie tried to put her hair up into something fashionable, but she knew it wasn't working. It had been hot the last few days of the trip. Parker told her they'd be at his place in a few hours, and she insisted he stop so she could wash her face and fix her hair.

She looked at the gray and blue dress she wore. It was her finest, yet it was best suited for use as dusters. Her skin had darkened due to the sun. She had one ladies' hat to wear, one made of woven straw that looked as though someone had ridden over it with a horse. Not only was the brim bent downward, but the dark blue ribbon that circled it and formed a wilted bow in back was frayed. She looked like a beggar. But she was clean. She twisted her hair one last time and secured it with her hair pins and then smiled. *One thing done.* She then set her crumpled hat on her head and secured it with a hat pin. Her shoes had seen better days, and she was lucky they hadn't just fallen apart.

There was no help for it. She was a Tennessee O'Rourke, after all. Swallowing down a laugh, she shook her head.

People would be waiting for them. Maxwell had ridden ahead to let Mrs. Eastman know of their pending arrival.

Climbing back to the front, she glanced at Parker. He looked so handsome in his clean clothes. His boots had such a shine on them.

"I'm nervous." She bit her lip.

He put his hand under her chin and brought his mouth down on hers. "Don't bite your lip. It'll be fine and I'll be there."

Giving him a weak smile, she nodded, but all the while her stomach churned. They started out and Georgie wished they had another day before she had to meet his mother. She was bound to think Georgie was not good enough for her son. What would she want to be called? Mother Eastman, Mother or by her first name?

"What is your mother's name?"

"Millicent Beauregard Eastman. Don't call her Millie, though, it makes her crazy." Parker patted her hand. "Look." He nodded his head to the front of them. "That's my ranch. Actually, I amend that. That's our ranch."

"Does it have a name?"

"The Eastman Ranch." Parker laughed. "My father was a straight shooter. He had a hard time imagining just how big he could make the ranch."

"But you have a vision of what you want." It wasn't a question it was a statement. "Oh my, the house is bigger than I pictured." She stared at the vast two story house. It looked elegant and not at all what she pictured a ranch house would look like.

"It's made of hand-hewn wood from the trees on the property. I built it with my father and Monty. We added the big porch to please Mother."

"It's exquisite, and I'm in awe that you built it. Many of

the men I knew before the war wouldn't risk getting calluses on their hands."

Parker laughed. "There were a few dandies around, weren't there? They ended up ill equipped for life in the army. But here we are. Oh look, Mother is waiting!"

Georgie's stomach clenched but she smiled at her husband's enthusiasm. He drove the wagon right up to the front of the house and reined in the horses. Then he jumped to the ground, immediately rounded the wagon, and helped her down. Smiling his encouragement, he took her hand, settled it in the crook of his elbow, and they walked up the steps together.

Millicent Beauregard Eastman took one look at her new daughter-in-law and gasped.

Georgie had known it was going to be that way, but it still hurt.

"Mother, may I present my bride, Georgie O'Rourke Eastman."

His mother opened her mouth then shut it. Her gaze swept Georgie up and down, and by the expression of disgust, she found her son's bride severely lacking. "You are Georgia O'Rourke? I think there has been some mistake. I meant, are you one of *the* O'Rourkes? The high-society O'Rourkes? Oh my, Parker, you didn't marry this chit did you?" Her eyes flashed in anger as she stared at her son.

"Yes, I just said she's my bride. I expect you to give her the respect my wife deserves. She is one of those O'Rourkes, but as you can see, much was lost in the war."

"You look more like a field hand than a wife. Look how dark you've allowed your skin to get. I hope you don't expect me to pay good money to make you look presentable. Didn't your mother tell you to bathe with lemons? Where is your maid?"

Georgie tilted her head up and ignored her mother-in-law. "Parker, I would like to rest a bit. Would you be so kind as to escort me to our room?"

Parker nodded.

Millicent gasped. "You will not sully my son by sharing a room with him."

Trying not to allow her gathering tears to fall, Georgie hurried into the house, with Parker right behind her. "Upstairs?"

"Yes. Georgie—"

"We can talk about it upstairs." She hated that her voice wobbled. Heck, she had stood up to the Union Army, but a few caustic words from Parker's mother was her undoing. She practically ran up the steps. "Which room?"

"I'm not sure. Mother wants us in separate rooms. Maybe she'll be kinder if we go along with her." Parker couldn't meet her gaze.

"You were a Captain in the Confederate Army. You are the head of this household. Where do *you* want me to sleep?"

He sighed loudly then opened a door and ushered her in. It wasn't his room. There was too much floral décor for it to be his room. Her heart dropped as she turned and stared at Parker. "You can't mean for me to stay in here."

He looked guilty and a bit sorry.

"Get out. I can't have you here right now. I thought you were a different type of man. I need to be alone for a while." She swallowed back her tears.

"I figured you'd like to be alone—"

"Close the door behind you," she said softly. As soon as the door shut, her tears fell. Where was the man she'd traveled with? He'd gone from a decisive, powerful man to a man who still hung onto his mother's skirts. Separate rooms would make it so she never had to... She'd never conceive a child. Disappointment overwhelmed her as she peered out the back window. She had a view of the bunkhouse but it was the view beyond that she found breathtaking. There was an abundance of green grass and plenty of trees. Cattle grazed as far as her eye could see. He'd be busy.

Turning from the window, she studied her surroundings. Her room in Tennessee was much bigger and much grander. This room consisted of a bed and wardrobe. There wasn't even a mirror. Just who did Millicent Beauregard Eastman think she was? She was nobody trying to be part of society.

But what did it matter? It didn't look as though anyone was willing to be Georgie's ally. She hadn't met everyone yet, but her hopes weren't high that she'd find anyone to stand up to Mother Eastman. Georgie shivered. That name would never do. That woman was no type of mother.

At a knock on the door, she opened it, hoping it was Parker with a different attitude. Her shoulders slumped at the sight of Maxwell with her few possessions. He looked around and gave her a look of pity before he stepped out and closed the door behind him.

If only she hadn't married Parker. Now she was tied to him forever. Or perhaps this *was* just an act to get his mother to accept her. She started to hang her few dresses in the wardrobe when the door flew open. Speak of the devil.

"Don't you dare put those disgraceful clothes in one of my wardrobes. I don't know what your game is, but I don't believe you're who you say you are. I talked to my son and an annulment is possible."

How could he have told his mother their private business? Her face burned. "Just what do you propose I wear?" Georgie cocked her right brow and gave her a haughty look.

"We're ready to sit down to dinner. I'll bring you something afterward. Come on, your *husband* is waiting." Millicent strode out of the room.

Georgie closed her eyes. What if she just refused to join them? Could she dare hope that Parker had some plan for the two of them? She followed at a slow pace and joined them in the dining room then stood next to her chair waiting for Parker to pull it out for her and after an uncomfortable length of time he finally stood and held it for her. She tried to catch his gaze but he had his face adverted the whole time. It felt like a knife slicing off a piece of her heart.

A man in cowboy garb served dinner. It was barely edible, but she managed to choke down a few bites. The utensils were silver-plated, not real silver, and the plates were made from inferior china. Millicent was a complete fake.

"You must have missed your son very much while he went to pick me up, Mother Eastman," Georgie stated with a smile. Millicent did not like being called Mother Eastman, and for some reason that brought Georgie a bit of pleasure.

"Georgia, you may call me Mrs. Eastman. And since we are talking about names, your name is Georgia not Georgie. I don't want to hear that hideous nickname again. It's beyond common."

"You may call me Mrs. Eastman too. And my father, Richard Alexander O'Rourke the fourth gave me that nickname. My mother, Mary Winston O'Rourke thought it was cute. So no it's not beyond common." She turned her head to look at her husband. "What do you think, Parker?"

He glanced at her and then at his mother. "Yes, Mrs. Eastman is fine. Truthfully, I was a little taken aback by the nickname, but I soon got used to it. Perhaps it was a fun childhood nickname but we all have to put our childhood behind us as we become adults. Georgia is such a pretty name, and it honors one of our great Southern states."

Georgie blinked once, twice, three times at him wondering where his backbone had gone.

"I'll be gone for two weeks or more. I have to check out the upper pastures and then go into town and check on our land deeds. People keep trying to steal my land. I also need to see what type of deal I can get for the cattle. Taggart and Stookey will stay behind and keep you both safe."

"Excuse me, I'm rather tired." Georgie wiped her mouth with the cloth napkin and then stood. There was no way she was asking permission. She wasn't sure what was going on but she was not going to acknowledge Mrs. Eastman's power. She wished she could weep about the loss of her husband. For that man sitting there was not the man she had married.

As she walked into her room, she noticed a clean white nightgown on her bed. She reached for it and frowned. It was made from cheap scratchy material. She'd worn worse, and she would not complain or let that woman know she was getting to her. She donned the gown and slipped into bed. Maybe when she woke up in the morning she'd find that this was all a horrible nightmare.

PARKER LEFT the dinner table and went outside to get some air. His mother was impossible, but he was afraid she'd get her whip out and use it on Georgie. He wouldn't be here to protect her. He'd talk to her tonight about it. He should have warned her.

He had seen his mother threaten the help with butcher knives before. He tried to get the doctor to help her, but the doc's suggestion was to keep her strapped to a chair during the day and the bed at night. Parker couldn't do that to his mother. She'd been back to normal when she talked about how Miss O'Rourke was coming to stay with them.

He waited outside until his mother's room lamp went out. His wife's lamp was still lit. Good, they needed to talk. He went inside as silently as he could and then snuck into Georgie's room.

No sooner had he entered than she sat straight up and opened her mouth.

"Shh," he warned urgently. "I need to talk to you, but I don't want to wake Mother." He hoped that Georgie would forgive him. He sat on the edge of the bed and met her angry expression. Did he look contrite enough? "I'm so sorry."

She tried to push him off the bed.

"My mother isn't well. I've been playing along with her for your sake."

She pulled the sheet up to her chin. "I don't believe you. You have been nothing but cruel to me since we got here. You are not the man I married, and I can't—I won't accept it. Your mother mentioned an annulment, and I think—"

He cut her off by kissing her, cradling the back of her head in his hand so she couldn't pull away. Almost immediately he felt her anger drain away, and he pulled her into his embrace. "I love you, Georgie."

She pulled back and stared into his eyes. "I don't believe you. I won't believe you."

"It's true. I didn't expect it, and I don't know how it happened so quickly, but I have deep feelings for you."

She shook her head violently. "I've been through too much to allow myself to be involved in whatever sick game you and your mother are playing. I plan to leave tomorrow." Tears filled her eyes.

"Oh Georgie, I need you to believe me. For some reason, my mother has gone a bit mad. It happened after the death of my father and brother. She took her anger out on the slaves, I heard. When I got back, the slaves were free but she didn't see it that way. She locked the two who worked in the house up at night. I made sure they weren't locked up, and I offered them wages. They left rather quickly, and I don't blame them." He swallowed hard. "I was so ashamed of her. Any help I hired she thought she could use a riding crop on. She even landed herself in jail at one point. The doctor suggested I tie her up day and night." He shook his head. "I just couldn't."

She dropped the sheet and took his hands in hers. "I'm so sorry."

He took a deep breath. "When she found you, she was herself again. She told me you were to be her companion."

Georgie dropped her chin to her chest and stared at their entwined hands.

"Hey, I'm not sorry I married you. I had Maxwell ride into town to get you ready made dresses and new shoes and stuff a woman needs. She'll be her old self again. Taggart and Stookey both promised to watch over you at all times. Don't worry about Taggart, he won't leer at you again."

He kissed the top of her head and then lifted her chin with his finger. "I don't want to force you, but she's positive we can get an annulment."

"You told her we never consummated the marriage."

"I did no such thing. I couldn't imagine talking to my mother about that."

She sighed. "I can't either. She must have been trying to find out if we did or didn't by guessing."

"I want to make you my wife in truth, Georgie. If something happens to me this would be your house. I don't want you to be homeless ever again." He leaned down and kissed her again. This time she wrapped her arms around his neck and drew him closer. His heart had never felt so full.

"Are you sure?"

"Yes. I love you too."

WHEN SHE WOKE the next morning, Parker wasn't in the bed with her. She smiled as she touched the pillow where she could still see an indentation from his head. He really did love her. She hopped up out of bed and ran to his room. She wanted to see him off.

Her new clothes were piled up on a large chair, and she smiled in delight. It had been years since she'd had new clothes. Quickly, she gathered what she needed and slipped on a dress in a shade of muted rose with a high collar made of lace in a cream color. She brushed her hair and added a pink ribbon to it. She didn't want to waste any time.

After she dashed down the stairs, she searched each room for Parker. Finally, she stepped outside.

"You're too late, you hussy. He didn't look rested when he left." Millicent peered at her and laughed. "You think that new clothes can hide what you really are? You somehow faked your name, married my boy, and then last night you made sure there would be no annulment. You can't fool me."

Georgie went back inside and made her way into the kitchen. It was a bit of a mess, and her hopes that there would be some breakfast rapidly faded. All that was there was a piece of bread. She ate it. What had happened to the cowboy from last night? She rolled up her sleeves, got hot water from the reserve tank on the stove, and poured it into the sink. The dishes weren't going to clean themselves.

When she was done, she went outside and checked the garden she'd glimpsed the day before. It needed weeding but it was well planted. A hat to keep the sun off her head would have been nice. She grabbed a towel from the kitchen and used it to kneel on. The morning went quickly, and she still had a ways to go. It would have to wait until the next morning when it was cooler out.

She picked some carrots and onions and found a few potatoes and brought them inside. Millicent stood there with a sour look on her face.

"Well what did you make for the noon meal? I don't see

anything, and I'm hungry. If you weren't so lazy you'd have made something."

"I can make some biscuits and heat up the leftover beef from last night if you'd like."

"Make it quick!" Millicent gave her a glare before she marched out of the kitchen.

A heavy sigh slipped out, and Georgie's shoulders sagged. This was going to be much harder than she had imagined. She made the noon meal only to have Millicent insist she wasn't hungry. Taggart and Stookey were happy to eat it at least. They usually ate in the bunkhouse, but all the men were out chasing down cattle and moving them to different pastures.

After she cleaned the dishes, she decided to put her new clothes away. Her heart sang in anticipation of opening all the packages. She hummed as she climbed the stairs and went into Parker's room. Her humming stopped as she stood there with her mouth hung open. Everything was gone. Immediately she went to the wardrobe and opened it but it was almost empty. She went into her room and opened that wardrobe. It contained two puritan looking dresses with aprons and her underthings. Her scratchy nightgown was there too. She pulled out the two dresses. They were identical, both brown and made with cheap cloth. They didn't have any adornments on them. There were two buttons in the back. They were also long sleeved. What was going on? Parker's mother must be mad in the head. Much madder than Parker had explained.

Should she confront the crazy lady or just let it be? Her first instinct was to throw the dresses at the bat crazy, woman but she decided that remaining calm would be the best bet. Millicent thought of her as a maid, not her son's wife. Did it make a difference? She'd be doing all the work

45

anyway. But it was maddening that the woman thought she could do this.

She still had the dress she was wearing. She'd have to hide it and find the other clothes. If she ignored the old lady, would that be for the best or would it make things worse? Why hadn't Parker stayed a few days longer?

She put the dresses back and closed the door to the wardrobe. She jumped when she realized that Millicent was in the room. She held a big knife in one hand and a crop in the other.

Georgie took a few steps back and took a deep breath. She'd stared down armies before but Millicent scared her. "What are you doing?" She tried to sound casual.

"Teaching you your place. Since you are of no use to me, you being a fake O'Rourke, you'll be my maid. I have certain expectations. One is that you wear your uniform. Put it on!" She took a menacing step toward Georgie.

The crazed look in her eye convinced Georgie to go along with it. "Sure, I can do that." Maybe she could find something to hit Millicent with but there wasn't anything in the bedroom. She took out one of the brown dresses and put it on with Millicent staring at her the whole time. She was no Southern lady.

"Hand me the dress you're wearing!"

Georgie hesitated before she handed her dress over. Millicent was going too far. But how to get the drop on her? Georgie would have to wait for an opportunity.

"Now the kitchen floor needs scrubbing before you chop wood and then make dinner. A decent dinner this time." Millicent smirked as she pretended to stab Georgie with the knife.

Swallowing hard, Georgie nodded and walked out of the room and down the stairs, fully aware of the threat of being stabbed at any time.

"Taggart, make sure she does the work we talked about. Use the crop I gave you on her. Do remember she is my son's wife so while you may beat her you can't touch her in a personal way. Got it?"

"Yes, ma'am." Taggart grinned as he eyed Georgie.

Georgie gasped. The gleam in Taggart's eyes didn't bode well for her. Stookey had to be around somewhere. He'd protect her. She didn't dare ask where he was. Instead, she went into the kitchen, rolled up her sleeves, filled a bucket with hot water, and added soap flakes to it. She got down on her hands and knees and scrubbed the wooden floor. It wasn't anything she hadn't done during the war. If Millicent thought to make her leave, she had another thought coming.

AN HOUR LATER, Georgie was finished. After standing and stretching, she dumped the dirty water outside and poured herself a glass of cool water.

"Thank you," Taggart laughed as he took the glass from her and drank it down. "No water for you. You'd best get to chopping the wood."

Georgie gave him her best glare and turned to go out the door when she felt the searing pain of the crop against her shoulder. The hurt took her breath away but she quickly recovered and walked outside. Her only satisfaction was she hadn't screamed.

There was more than enough chopped wood piled against the house. This chore was punishment. She looked for a pair of gloves as she picked up the axe. There weren't any. For a moment, she thought to use the axe on Taggart but he carried a sidearm. There wasn't any choice but to do the work.

It wasn't the first time she'd chopped wood but the calluses she'd built up had disappeared and it was going to

47

hurt like hell. She put a log on the chopping block, raised the axe, and cut the wood in half. Then she needed to cut the two halves into new halves. She chopped for well over an hour she figured, according to the position of the sun. Now she had to stack it. It wasn't the work that made her mad, though. It was Taggart watching her that did. He was the lowest type of man.

"Where is Stookey?" she asked.

"He'll be gone by tomorrow. Mrs. Eastman fired him." Taggart smiled smugly as though he found great pleasure in Stookey's misfortune.

She made sure to keep her expression unchanged. Taggart would get no satisfaction from her. She walked to the water pump and washed her hands. She cupped water in her hand and drank some. She jumped at the excruciating sting that assaulted her other shoulder. Closing her eyes, she tried to breathe through her pain. She straightened up nice and tall, lifted her chin a bit, and walked inside.

She found some beans that had soaked overnight, perhaps left by the cowboy who had cooked their dinner, and now they were soft enough to cook. She went down into the root cellar. The door to the root cellar was a panel in the floor of the large pantry. There wasn't much down there just lamp oil and a few lamps. She frowned as her eyes adjusted to the dark. Parker would know better than to allow the root cellar to be empty. She'd have to get canning anything and everything. Why weren't they prepared for an Indian attack or a tornado? Union Soldiers would certainly be enough of a reason to fill it to the brim.

The panel fell closed and she was sent into pitch darkness. She went to the steps and tried to push the panel up. She heard Taggart laugh. What was wrong with him? The dark had been her friend more than once, so she didn't care. She sat down and prayed for a while. She prayed for all the people who were homeless and all the folks who had lost loved ones. She prayed for Parker's safety and for Millicent's madness to go away. If only she had an escape plan. Between Millicent and Taggart, she could very well be dead by the time Parker returned.

If he really loved her, he wouldn't have left her with his mother and Taggart. It was a very poor choice and he'd had to have known it.

"Who is going to cook dinner? You Taggart? Do you know how to cook?" Millicent screeched.

Instantly, the panel was opened. Georgie acted as though nothing was amiss. She climbed out and put more wood in the cook stove. She then put the beans on the top of it and after that, she walked out the door.

A smile tugged at her lips when she heard Taggart cursing to keep up with her. She opened the door to the smokehouse that she had found while exploring earlier and used the sharp knife inside of it to cut off a hunk of pork. She put the knife back down, careful to keep her movements casual, as though the knife were of no consequence, but it was wonderful to know where one was kept. Then she hurried to the house, set the pork on the counter, and after grabbing a basket, she hurried back outside.

She took a moment to pull more weeds before she pulled up an onion and two carrots. Some creeping plants off to one side yielded a lot of green beans. She took a moment to wipe the perspiration from her brow before going back inside to make dinner.

Taggart sat at the small table looking bored. Well, too bad. He'd probably thought it would be fun to guard her, but he was finding out differently.

Her feet hurt, but she didn't sit to snap off the ends of the beans. Back in Tennessee, they ate the whole thing if they were even lucky enough to find green beans. She had planted a garden in the woods, out of sight. It didn't matter which army came, they always pillaged for food. In the woods, so many animals had ravaged her garden but she'd been able to feed herself and many of the freedmen, though their meals had been very meager.

Everything went into the pot, and she stirred it. Then she got busy making corn bread. Tomorrow she'd need to gather eggs and find out if there was a milk cow nearby. They were nearly out of both. There were more than enough chores to do that chopping unneeded wood was just crazy.

Her hands were a bloody mess and they pained her, so she nearly cried in relief when she discovered a basket in the pantry with medical supplies. She took the basket and set it on the table. After she pulled out a roll of cloth bandages and set it next to the basket she hunted for some salve. There wasn't any. She gently wrapped her blisters. It didn't help much, but it would give them a bit of protection.

She stood to return the basket when Taggart grabbed her arm, hard. "I don't ever want to see scissors in your hand again. You ask for permission. Got it?"

The grip he had on her arm hurt and she could picture the bruise he'd leave on her. "I got it."

"The table needs to be set, Georgia!" Millicent called from the front room.

There was simply no end. Georgie walked into the dining room and began to set the table but Millicent came in and proceeded to show her the errors of her ways.

"Only two plates, one for me and one for Mr. Taggart."

"And Mr. Stookey? Where is he going to eat?"

Millicent shrugged her shoulders. "In the bunk house, I suppose. You can bring him one bowl. As for you, you're to eat in the kitchen as your station in life dictates."

"My station? I'm your son's wife and an O'Rourke. I do believe I have some relations in Texas. I'll need to get in touch with them. But never mind, I'd rather eat alone." She turned and immediately felt the leather thongs of the crop bite into her neck and under her chin. She almost doubled over. Millicent had used every bit of her strength.

When Georgie touched her neck, she encountered wetness and when she lowered her hand, blood was on her fingers. There was no way she'd stay. Perhaps Stookey could help her. Her body shook as she walked back into the kitchen.

After serving Millicent and Taggart their meal, she stole into Parker's study and sat behind his desk. She looked for something to write with. She found parchment paper and ink. She dipped the quill she'd also found and wrote her husband a letter.

Dear Husband

I hope all is well with you. Other arrangements need to be made here at the house. Your mother took away my clothes and left me with a maid's clothing. She has Taggart guard me as I do chore after chore. I had to chop wood today. We already had plenty of wood. Taggart hit me twice with the crop and your mother hit me on my neck and under my chin, drawing blood. I'm hoping I won't be left with scars. I'm happy to do chores but not when I'm whipped.

Stookey has been fired. I have no one to defend me. I hope you receive this letter because I'm pinning all my hope on you.

Your Faithful Wife

Georgie

SHE HURRIEDLY PUT everything back where it was and tucked the sealed letter in her apron pocket. Then she snuck back into the kitchen. Could she possibly take the crop away from Taggart? Her heart sunk. He'd been a soldier, and he'd punish her if he even knew she was considering it. She hurried into the dining room and gave them both seconds before she brought Stookey his meal.

She gasped loudly. He was curled up into a ball on a bunk. She put the food on the table and then went to his side. "Mr. Stookey? Oh, Stookey, what have they done to you?" She only saw half of his face but his eye was swollen closed. Blood had dried around his nose and mouth. Even his neck had bruises on it. She touched his back and he cried out in pain.

Tears filled her eyes. "I'm so sorry about this. I'm going to slip a letter I want posted into your saddlebag. Then I'm going to get a few supplies to help you to feel better. I'll be right back."

Enraged, she ran to the house, intent on confronting Taggart, but he stood at the door waiting for her.

"You are not to leave this house without my permission! Get in here. I'm going to make sure you never forget to ask."

"Taggart, please I need to tend to Stookey. He's in a bad way."

Taggart laughed at her. "You need to worry about yourself. Lean over the table!"

She shook her head and took a step back. "No."

"Oh yes." He grabbed her and pushed her down onto the table. "If you move, I'll make it so you can't walk."

He took out the crop and hit her over and over. There wasn't a place he missed. Her back, bottom, and thighs were lashed. She couldn't help but cry out and scream, even though it was useless. No one would rescue her. She sobbed and just when she thought she was going to pass out, he stopped. He shoved her off the table and she hit the floor hard. Then he we walked out, leaving her where she had fallen.

Moving was near impossible, but she did it. She stood and besides the excruciating agony caused by her injuries, she was dizzy. How far was the nearest neighbor? Where was the nearest town? Why hadn't she asked Parker before he'd left? She needed to find her relations. They lived South of Fort Worth, but she didn't know exactly where Fort Worth was. She hobbled into Parker's study and locked the door. It took a long time but she managed to jam a chair under the doorknob.

The beautiful amber color of the whiskey on the sideboard called to her. She poured herself a little and drank it down. It burned a bit, but it eased her pain some. She poured much more into a glass and carried the glass and decanter to the sofa, setting both on one of the side tables. She grabbed the blanket that hung over the back of the sofa. Everything she did brought more hurt. Next, she made sure the window shutters were secured on the inside.

Taking a few more swigs of the whiskey, she took off her dreadful maid's dress. She had to get all her clothes off or they would stick to the blood, and getting them off after that would be too much to bear. Her stomach churned as she forced herself to drink more whiskey, but it was helping with the pain. Finally, she lay on her stomach and slept.

CHAPTER FOUR

For two days, Taggart and Millicent tried to get her out of the study. She didn't bother to answer them. At one point, she heard Millicent ask Taggart if Georgia was dead. They even broke the window but the shutters wouldn't allow entrance. The house was superbly made. The only things she lacked were food and water. She found bottles of whiskey in a closet but no food. It didn't matter. She wasn't very hungry anyway.

She wanted to laugh, but she knew if she started she'd grow hysterical and never stop. She had survived the Union Army and stood her ground with the Confederates and every other person who thought they could take advantage of her. Then when the Yankees burned the house, she'd survived that too. Unfortunately, she'd been the only surviving member of her family that awful day.

With God's help, she had made it through and was able to help others in need. Now here she was being hunted by a crazy woman and her henchman. She rubbed her hand across the mahogany desk. Parker must have had some inkling of what he left her to face. She sat in his chair and dropped her face in her hands. The motion brought on a surge of throbbing and stinging, and she let out a whimper. But pain was the least of her worries. Soon she'd need food.

Her search for a weapon had been futile. Who didn't keep a gun in their desk drawer? She prayed that Stookey was able to heal up and get her letter to Parker. She really had no idea where her husband was. The more she thought about it, the more she feared that she'd displeased him the night before he left. It added up. He hadn't even said goodbye to her. It didn't make any sense that he'd leave her with Taggart. He'd seen the way the man looked at her when they'd come upon them along the journey here.

The betrayal sliced her heart. He obviously didn't love her, so why say he did? Had he thought she'd be able to handle his mother? He didn't seem to even know how mad his mother really was. There hadn't been a single visitor paying Millicent a social call during the four or so days Georgie had been there.

It was growing dark outside. She waited until she heard two bedroom doors close. Now would be the time to grab some food and water. Then she'd search the study for a map. Her head had been too fuzzy from the spirits she drank to do it earlier.

Not daring to light a lamp, she tiptoed out to the hall and then on to the kitchen. As quietly as she could she gathered provisions to last her a few weeks. Then she took the pitcher of water. Carefully she returned to the study. She locked the door and shoved the chair under the doorknob again. She went to the sideboard to sort her bounty when she heard Taggart clear his throat.

She whirled around and faced him. He was well hidden in the shadows. Fear coursed through her, and her body trembled.

"You sure thought you had me outwitted. You made me

look like a buffoon who couldn't handle a slip of a woman. I'm so tempted to show you who's in charge but Mrs. Eastman wouldn't like it. I have a good job here and I plan to keep it as long as possible. I do have some sad news for you. Stookey died and he wasn't able to pass along your letter. Poor Stookey, he didn't know how to mind his own business."

She felt the blood drain from her face. "He's dead?" Her heart thumped painfully against her chest. She inched her way toward the door.

"Where do you think you're going?" The amusement in his voice angered her.

"I might as well sleep in my own bed." All she wore was her shift, and she wanted to get to her room before Taggart decided to light a lamp.

"Fine, but I'll be right behind you. I have to take off the door. You can't be trusted."

She walked out of the study. Her back hurt with each step, but somehow she managed to make it up the stairs and into her room. She lay in her bed and covered herself as she watched Taggart remove her door. She didn't care anymore; in fact, that might make it easier to sneak out.

When he finished, he stared at her. "I bet the Captain had a high old time breaking you in before he left. Must have hurt. There was a lot of blood on the sheets." He snickered before he left.

If it was the last thing she did, she'd get revenge and Taggart would be made to suffer. She'd have to sleep in her shift. It was already beginning to stick to her broken skin.

Six weeks after leaving his new wife asleep in their marriage bed, Parker had finally inspected his entire ranch and made it to town where he would finish up with some business. He was just leaving his lawyer's office with maps and titles to all of his holdings. No one was going to take his land. They'd found a homesteader building a house on his property. The homesteader hadn't bothered to make a claim or pay for the land.

Parker had a few of his men disassemble the house. He'd given the man one week to get off his land. He left two of his men there to make sure it got done. Parker had thought that when the war was over there wouldn't be a need always have a gun strapped on but it was a necessity.

"Mr. Eastman! Yoo hoo, Mr. Eastman, I have to talk to you!" A stout woman in her thirties came running down the boardwalk. As she got closer, he recognized her as Mrs. Bowman. She'd tried to help with his mother, but it hadn't worked out.

He nodded his head. "Mrs. Bowman, slow down. What can I do for you?"

Her breathing was labored and she put a hand to her chest. "You're needed at home. A man named Mr. Stookey is dead, and your poor wife has fallen ill."

Fear clutched him. "What? Wait, slow down."

"Mr. Stookey's body was found in a ravine, and someone remembered he'd been under your command in the war. How they figured out it was him, I'll never know. The Commander here took his Union troops out to your place, and found your wife in bed burning up with fever. He sent a doctor out. I haven't heard anything else."

He reached out and gave her arm a quick squeeze. "Thank you." He raced through the street to his horse, yelling for his men to follow him.

Stookey dead? Were Taggart and his mother sick too? Stookey had always been a bit shy but he'd been a good soldier. And Taggart had proven his loyalty again and again.

"What's up?" Maxwell asked as he caught up to Parker.

"Stookey is dead and Georgie is sick. I hope she's still alive when I get there."

"What about your mother and Taggart?"

Parker shook his head. "I don't know."

It was one of the longest rides of his life. He prayed the whole way. Georgie couldn't die.

Finally, the house was in view. Parker barely slowed his horse before he jumped down and ran into the house. He was stunned that his mother and Taggart sat in the dining room eating.

"Where is she?" he demanded.

"Before you go up to her, you need to know she's prone to making up stories—" Taggart started to get to his feet, but Parker pinned him down with a harsh glare.

He took the steps two at a time and the smell coming from her room was nauseating. He expected to find her dead body, but she was alive. She looked so very tiny in the bed. He rushed to her side and was shocked at how sunken her eyes were.

"Georgie?"

Her eyes flickered open for a moment, and they seemed unusually bright. "My name is Georgia. Please I can't afford to get into more trouble." Her eyes closed and her head rolled to the side.

Parker touched her forehead and sure enough, she was burning up. He looked around for water and a cloth but they weren't there.

"Maxwell!" Parker called when he heard the sound of Maxwell's boots coming up the steps. "I need a pail of cold water and as many cloths and towels as you can find. She's burning up."

Parker pulled back the sheets on the bed and found them to be soiled. He seethed. There seemed to be blood too. He cut off her chemise and cursed. The whip marks were numerous and they crisscrossed from her neck down. He ached for her. He went to lift her but the soiled sheet stuck to her body. How? Why? He covered her with a clean sheet he found in the wardrobe.

"Got what you need. Here you go..." Maxwell's mouth dropped open, and his eyes filled with despair.

Parker took the bucket and put it on the table next to the bed and wet a cloth. He wiped her forehead, but she didn't respond.

"First we have to get her cleaned up." He shot a meaningful look at the other man. "*Never* tell her you saw her without clothes on."

"I promise," Maxwell vowed.

Parker kept her as covered as he could while he showed Maxwell the sheet. "We'll have to wet the sheet and hope it doesn't hurt too much as we peel it away from her skin." Parker swallowed hard. He was going to kill Taggart.

Together they wet the sheet and peeled as gently as they could. She cried out, but her eyes didn't open. Both men had tears in their eyes as they worked.

Parker opened the window and threw the chemise, dirty sheet, and used cloths out the window. The he turned her onto her stomach and cleaned her the best he could.

"I'll get the salve I have in my saddlebag," Maxwell said as he hurried from the room.

Parker continued to wash her down as gently as he could. The slashes from the whip were angry and red, and some had become festered; they went all the way to her knees. He put the clean sheet over her for a moment and kissed her temple. "I'm so sorry, Georgie. How could they have done this to you?"

She opened her eyes. "I fought with everything I had, but I didn't win." Tears seeped down her face. "It started the day you left and only got worse. I can't bear the pain. Please no more pain."

His heart ached. "I'll find something to help with it."

"The doc gave them laudanum, but they wouldn't give it to me." Her voice was barely audible.

"I'll be right back."

Parker ran down the steps intent on beating Taggart, but only his mother was sitting at the table. "Where's Taggart?"

"He said he had somewhere to be." She seemed unconcerned.

"Where is the medicine the doctor gave her?" Parker thought he'd snap.

"Why, it's on the kitchen counter, dear."

He glared at his mother and hurried into the kitchen. He grabbed the full bottle, a spoon, and filled a glass with water.

"Are you going to give that to her? What about the baby? It can't be good for the baby."

God, I need your help. He went back upstairs. He stood at the door for a moment. She hadn't looked the least bit pregnant. But he'd have to ask before he gave her the medicine.

Maxwell was slathering the salve on her back and legs. When Parker put the medicine, water, and spoon on the table, Maxwell handed him the jar. "Here, you do the rest. It isn't right for me to touch her that way."

Parker nodded and took the salve. Maxwell went to the window and stared out. Parker rubbed the salve on Georgie, and he wasn't sure if he would have survived such a beating. She hardly cried out. He finished, and it was time to ask her.

He covered her with the sheet again and the knelt on the floor so he could see her eyes. "Georgie, I have to ask you something. Are you pregnant?"

Her wails of grief tore through him. He wished he could take her into his arms but he'd only end up hurting her. She sobbed so hard he was afraid she'd make herself sicker.

"Please, I need to know before I give you the medicine." He stroked her hair and then her cheek.

"There's no need for you to worry about another mouth to feed. I barely knew I was with child before it was beaten out of me. There isn't a baby anymore." Her voice shook with despair.

Parker glanced at Maxwell and saw anger on the other man's face. "Find Taggart. No not you, I need you with me. Send four of the men, and I want him alive."

He didn't even hear Maxwell leave. He was too focused on his wife. "I'm going to need you to hold up your head so I can give you the laudanum, my love."

She stiffened when he said "my love," and he could only guess what those two monsters had told her.

He poured the medicine onto the spoon and carefully put it in Georgie's mouth. He followed it with a few sips of water.

"I'm going to move you to my room. The room you should have been in from day one. It's going to hurt a bit, but it's clean and it has a door." He sure as heck was going to find out why the door was gone.

Gently, he lifted her. She weighed hardly anything, and when he looked, he could see her ribs. He wouldn't blame her if she hated him. He carried her across the hall and set her on the big, clean bed in his room. He used more of the cool water and a clean cloth to try to keep her fever down. Guilt ate at him. He should have guessed that this would have happened. He'd known his mother was mad, but he hadn't realized she would go this far. And now they had killed his child, *their* child, and they'd almost killed his wife.

He strode to his window overlooking the front of the property, opened it, and shouted for someone to go and get the doctor. Two of his cowboys instantly mounted up and headed for town. Glancing over his shoulder, he noted his wife in peaceful slumber and sighed. Next he took off his boots and lay on the bed beside her, being careful not to touch her.

He was the protector, and he had failed to protect what was most precious to him. He hadn't been too keen on having to marry her, but he had missed her terribly while he was gone. His eyes misted. They would have had a child if not for his inept decision to leave her with his mother. He'd just been so hopeful they would get along, that Georgie would be able to reach his mother in her madness and bring back the woman she had once been. Had the babe been a boy or a girl? They probably didn't know. She had lost it—no it had been murdered—early in the pregnancy. Would there be other children?

Georgie whimpered in her sleep, and he stroked her hair and the side of her face. That calmed her. It was going to take a long while to get her trust back. She hadn't given it lightly the first time. Hopefully, there was still a chance for them.

Praise be to the God and Father of our Lord Jesus Christ, the Father of compassion and the God of all comfort, who comforts us in all our troubles, so that we can comfort those in any trouble with the comfort we ourselves receive from God.

He remembered that passage from the bible and it was fitting. With God's help, he'd be able to comfort Georgie. Parker's heart felt lighter and a sense of peace washed over him.

GEORGIE OPENED her eyes and cautiously peered at her surroundings. She was in Parker's room. He must have come home. For some reason, she'd thought it a dream. Bless him, he must have bathed her. She had a soft nightgown on. The pain was so bad she wanted to weep, but she wouldn't just in case Parker had left. Taggart couldn't abide tears, and his reaction to them was to use the crop on her. There wasn't a spot on her back that didn't sear with pain. She could only imagine what it must look like.

Did Parker know about the baby? Her heart squeezed, and as hard as she tried not to, tears trailed down her face, making her pillow wet. She'd had such high hopes for a life here with Parker, but it wasn't to be.

She heard two sets of boots on the stairs and tensed, only making her agony worse. She turned her head, though she didn't truly want to know who was coming in the door. It didn't matter. In fact, nothing mattered except getting strong enough to leave.

When the doctor came into view, she cringed. He'd been summoned when she'd started losing the baby. He hadn't been any help, and he obviously hadn't reported what was happening to the sheriff. All he'd said was there was always next time. She hadn't wanted to hear about next time. She wanted to grieve the baby she'd just lost.

He reached out and touched her forehead, and she turned her head away from him. She found herself looking right into Parker's eyes. The sorrow she saw reflected her own suffering. Maybe he understood her grief. She wanted to turn away from him but she couldn't look at the doctor. She just couldn't.

"What do you think, Doc? Has her fever gone down?" Parker sounded hopeful.

"You and your friend, stripping her down and washing her with cold water must have helped."

"You're not leaving are you? You haven't checked her back, and what about her, er, where babies come out? I don't want any infections setting in. She'd been lying in filth for days. There was still blood on the sheet from the miscarriage."

"I blame your man and your mother. I gave them strict instructions to keep her wounds clean. Now, looking at her, she could use some water. If she can keep it down, give her tea and broth. Start slow. I don't know when she last ate. Has she always been this thin?"

"If you'll step outside, I'll take her gown off so you can examine her back."

She heard the door close. "Please, Parker, the pain is too much to bear."

"I know, love. I've got your laudanum right here."

She watched as he poured some of the liquid onto the spoon and helped her to get her head up far enough so as not to spill it. He also had her sip some water afterward. He then carefully took her gown off. She bit her bottom lip hard to keep from screaming.

"That doctor is useless. He saw the conditions I was being kept in and never said a word. He could have alerted the sheriff, but he didn't." She shifted and hissed through her teeth as the throbbing sting increased. "He didn't put anything on my back. I'm not sure if he even looked at it. He just made sure everything about the baby came out of my body. It was humiliating to have everyone watching."

Parker closed his eyes and winced. Then he opened his eyes and they were full of anger. "Let's just have him look at your back. Then I'm going to pull him out of the house by his ear. I know a woman I can ask to come and make sure the other part of you is fine."

She should be grateful, but why hadn't he used such care when he'd left Taggart behind to watch over her? And Parker's mother needed to be locked away, but he'd left without so much as a warning regarding how mentally damaged she was. He was her husband, but Georgie couldn't help the rage building inside of her.

Parker opened the door and let the doctor in. She just

closed her eyes and tried to think of something pleasant but not much came to mind. When she'd discovered she was having a baby that had been the best day. She'd found hope. But now here she was. All of her joy had been cruelly taken from her.

Hasten, O God, to save me; come quickly, LORD, to help me. She repeated those words over and over in her mind. It was the only way she obtained peace.

The laudanum and her prayers calmed her, and she jumped when Parker shoved the doctor out of the room and slammed the door while the doctor was still sputtering excuses.

"He didn't think any of the stitches were necessary."

"Stitches? I don't have stitches."

He sat on the bed next to her. "A few of your lashes were rather deep so I cleaned them and then stitched them. You were sleeping."

"I trust your judgement more than the doctor's. Most of the pain has faded away for a while. I keep asking myself what crime I committed to deserve what happened to me. The worst part was losing the baby. I took their punishments, but while I was lying in pain, I'd think about how happy you'd be when I told you. I'm so sad about it, and I can't seem to shake it. No more babies."

Parker lay on the bed so they were eye to eye. "Is that what the doctor said? Are you unable now? I'll get Mrs. Hanks here this afternoon to make sure you're all right."

"No, the doctor didn't say I couldn't. I just can't go through that again."

He took her hand and rubbed the back of it with his thumb. "Next time will be different."

"I'm not sure it will be. It came to be that it didn't matter if I broke some nonsensible rule or not. I still got whipped. I'm a nervous wreck."

"I wish I had done things differently. I am so sorry, Georgie."

She didn't know what to say so she was silent. He kissed her cheek. "I'm going to send for Mrs. Hanks. She's a midwife. I'll be right back."

She tried to give him a small smile. She tried hard, but it wouldn't come. She closed her eyes, the medicine made her so sleepy.

AT THE SOUND OF VOICES, Georgie opened her eyes. Her eyes widened, and she closed her legs. "What are you doing?" Her voice trembled and her body began to shake.

Parker came to her side. "Mrs. Hanks was examining you."

Georgie peered down to the end of the bed and saw a kindly looking woman with white hair and a youthful spark in her brown eyes. "What do you think, Mrs. Hanks?"

Mrs. Hanks set Georgie's nightgown to rights and pulled the sheet up to her neck again. Then she put her hand on Georgie's forehead and smiled. "You'll be fine. Let's get you turned over. You must be in pain lying on your back. Would you mind awfully if we took your gown off. The air will help you to heal better."

Georgie turned toward Parker. She still felt a bit confused from the medicine. "What do you think?"

"I think we should do what Mrs. Hanks suggests. I'll be the only one in and out of this room. No one will see you."

She nodded and allowed them both to slip the gown off her back.

"Did the doctor give you anything to put on your back?" Mrs. Hanks asked her. Georgie liked that Parker wasn't the one she asked.

"No, he's not much of a doctor. At first we put some salve on it, but I think it's all gone."

"I'll have my daughter Fiona drop some off for you. Put it on every morning and every evening. It'll help with the scarring too. Leave your windows open and allow the air to heal you. If you're cold you could build a fire or your husband probably has enough body heat for both of you." She patted Georgie on the hand. "Now let's turn you."

Georgie concentrated on not screaming, and finally she lay on her stomach again. Her eyes closed. She was so tired.

"You're going to have to do something about your mother. This is criminal what she did and what she allowed. I don't think it's safe to keep her here unless you lock her in her room. I don't know what else to tell you."

"I know. It's just so hard. Let me rephrase that. It *was* hard, but after what she did to my wife I now know she's totally out of her mind. I'll look into the options, Mrs. Hanks. Thank you so much for all your help."

"You send someone if you need me. I hate to speak ill of anyone, but that doctor just doesn't care."

"Let me walk you out," Parker said.

CHAPTER FIVE

*P*arker was at his wits' end. How was he going to get Georgie to talk to him again, really talk to him? She replied to his questions with one-word answers. He missed her. He missed the closeness they had built between them. It had been three weeks since Mrs. Hanks had come to check on Georgie. The air did help the wounds to heal, the physical ones at least.

Parker helped Georgie dress and then carried her downstairs each morning. He'd hired a sweet woman named Sondra to cook and clean and to take care of his mother, who was locked in her room. He'd had the wall between her room and the empty one next to hers taken down so she'd have a bigger place to live in. He'd had a few layers of quilt batting nailed to the walls to muffle her screams.

He'd have to put her in an asylum. The screams only seemed to take Georgie back to the mistreatment she'd endured. The angry outbursts were the worst. As his mother's rage-filled shrieks filtered through the walls, Georgie shook and cringed. One time he found her huddled under their bed. It had brought tears to his eyes. She'd endured such terrible hardships during the war, and it was his mother who had finally broken her.

Meanwhile, he wasn't getting as much work done as he would have liked. He'd hired more cowboys to help out.

He headed upstairs, intending to help Georgie get dressed. Dismay filled him when he found her rolled up into a ball under the blankets. It was shocking how pale she looked. Sighing, he took his boots off, climbed into the bed, and slipped under the blankets.

Taking her into his arms, he tried to soothe her. After a while, she lay with her head on his chest. He was able to pull the blankets down off their heads. He put his arms around her and held her tight.

"Would you like to take a walk with me?" he asked.

"No."

Here they went with the one word responses. "Is there anything else you'd like to do?"

"I want… I want to ride a horse and feel the wind on my face." She lifted her head and stared at him. Her eyes looked so hopeful.

"I'm not sure you're healed up enough. I could get the wagon and we could go for a ride that way."

"No. I want to ride with you. I want your arms keeping me safe as we ride. I need to regain myself but it's going so slowly I'm afraid I'm lost."

It was the most interested in life and living he had seen her in days. He had to give in. "I'll help you Georgie, my love. Let's get you dressed."

"In a minute. I want to lie here with you. You make me feel safe again."

He smiled at her. "I'll always be here for you."

She laid her head on his chest again. "I appreciate it. I need to be able to stand strong on my own two feet again. Half the time I'm scared. I know your mother is locked up, but still I'm afraid she'll get out and come for me. She carried a long knife with her the whole time you were gone. I thought for sure you'd find me with my throat cut."

"I'm looking for a place to put her. I've had inquiries sent out."

She scooted up and kissed him tenderly. His heart ached at the sweetness of it.

"Well I'm going to get dressed." She got out of bed on her own and selected an emerald green dress from her wardrobe. "You know I'm glad most women have done away with wearing corsets. It makes things much easier."

Easier for her perhaps but knowing how easily he could undress her was becoming a problem for him. Three more weeks. That was how long Mrs. Hanks had said to wait. It was going to be a long three weeks.

He got out of bed and buttoned Georgie's dress. "Let me get your stockings."

"I can do it. Put your boots on."

While putting on his boots, he watched her put on her stockings and shoes. From the way she moved, her back was healing well. If only he could get her mind to heal as well. He'd seen reactions like hers from soldiers who'd seen too much death and destruction.

"You look lovely. Would you like to come to the barn with me?"

Her chin wobbled for a moment before she nodded. She grabbed his hand and entwined their fingers. Instantly his breath caught.

He led her into the barn and stopped at the first stall. She seemed hesitant.

"This is Mine. She's the best mare I have."

Georgie smiled. "What's her name?" She reached out and petted the side of her face.

"Her name is Mine."

She chuckled softly, and the sound lifted his heart.

"I'll get her saddled."

"What type of horse is she?"

"She's a mix. I know she has some Arabian in her because of her smaller face. With her dark brown coloring, I just call her a bay. Whatever her mix is, she's fast and she has stamina." He was proud of his mare. She'd gotten him out of tough spots before. He grabbed the tack and saddle and got Mine ready.

He led his horse outside and lifted Georgie onto the front part of the saddle. "Does it hurt at all?"

"No."

Back to one-word answers. He put his foot in the stirrup and carefully hauled himself into the saddle behind his wife. He had her sitting sideways. He wasn't going to take a chance of her riding astride and hurting anything important. He pulled her back so she was practically sitting on his lap.

"How about now?" He waited for a yes or no.

"It feels very nice." She leaned against him and sighed in what sounded like contentment.

He kicked Mine's sides, and off they went. He started off at a walk and then urged Mine into a canter, heading toward a wooded part of his property where they'd be guaranteed privacy. Slowing Mine to a walk, he guided her down a trail that led to a stream. "I think you'll like this place."

"I'm sure I will." Georgie actually sounded enthusiastic. Maybe things were better already. Having her in his arms felt so wonderful, so right.

"Oh! Look a stream. Can we stop?"

He laughed. "Of course." He swung down and gently reached up for her. It made his heart skip a beat as she slid down his body and wrapped her arms around his neck, pulling him down for a kiss. It started sweet, but she deepened it. The kiss took him off guard, but he was willing to just go with it. Too soon she let go and turned toward the stream.

"I hope you don't think me too wanton." The back of her neck grew red.

"No. We're married. There is nothing wrong when it's between man and wife. I quite enjoyed it."

She glanced over her shoulder at him and smiled. "I'm taking off my shoes and hose. I want to go wading. I used to go wading all the time, before life became hard." Her smile faded but she turned back and found a fallen tree to use as a bench. She was soon ready to go wading and she laughed as she stepped in.

"It's colder than I thought it would be!" She splashed the water with her feet. "Join me!"

Normally he'd refuse, but he'd do anything to see her happy. He made quick work of taking off his boots and socks. He then rolled up his pants. He stuck on toe in. "It's too cold."

"Oh my! You get in here!"

Grinning at her, he stepped into the water, and almost instantly his feet went numb. Jumping onto one foot then the other and back again, he eventually grew used to the temperature of the water. "Tell me it's not cold."

Her eyelashes fluttered as her smile grew impish. "It's not cold."

In one long stride, he grabbed her up into his arms intent on teasing her, but she froze and her body shook.

Letting her go, his heart dropped. "I didn't mean to upset you."

She swallowed hard. "I'm fine." She smiled, but it was fake.

He wasn't sure what to do. Should he pretend to accept her fake smile? Should he get out? Perhaps he should take her home. The next thing he knew she pushed him and he fell.

The icy water rushed over him, soaking his trousers in seconds. Sitting in the water, he laughed at her wide-eyed expression.

"Don't you want to sit on my lap?" he teased.

"I think I'll pass. You know what? I do believe this water is a bit chilly for me. I can hardly feel my feet anymore." She quickly scrambled out of the stream.

"You are so right. I have certain parts on me I can't feel anymore either." He stood and walked to the bank. Water dripped off him and formed little puddles at his feet. "I guess the only thing to do is to take my trousers off and put them in the sun to dry. Oh, and my smalls are wet too."

He waited for her to protest but she just shifted from one foot to the other. Then she took Mine's reins.

"Come on, Mine. We need to get out of these woods and find the sun." She glanced over at Parker. "Are you coming?"

"I'm right behind you." If only he could read her mind, he'd be fine.

She found a spot that was both grassy and sunny and then stopped. Next, she took the bedroll he always carried off the saddle and handed it to him. "I'll turn around so you can take off whatever needs to be dried. Then I'll lay them out for you."

His lips twitched and he hurried to get his clothes off. He covered his lower half with a blanket. "You can lay out my clothes now."

She peeked first before she turned around. After she put his clothes to dry, she sat next to him. "At least your shirt is still dry."

"Yes, there is that."

"You're mad at me."

Laughter bubbled up in him and it took a bit before he could stop. "My love, why would I be mad? We were having fun. I had a little less fun than you is all."

"I did have fun."

After he put his arm around her, he drew her close. "I'm sorry I upset you by grabbing you."

"You didn't do anything wrong. I just reacted, and I can't seem to help it. I think they had me on edge for so long, it's hard for me to relax. I want to be playful and have fun but sometimes I just freeze in fear. I hope it goes away." She stared at the horizon.

"You blame me, don't you?" He held his breath.

"At first I lay all the blame at your feet. You left Taggart here. I figured you must have known what type of man he was. But I heard he'd always been a good soldier and even saved your life. I hated you because my baby died. I wanted to kill you for how your mother treated me. But after you came home, I came to hate you less and less. I honestly don't hate you any longer. You make me feel protected."

The words he wanted to hear weren't said. He wanted to hear that she loved him. "There was a time I thought you loved me."

She was silent for a long while. "I don't know if I know how to love anymore. I feel as though that part of me is broken. I'll be a good wife to you, Parker. We only have three more weeks, and then you can bed me. You'll have to go slow and gently at first. I don't want to end up giving you a black eye." She snuggled against him. "I know that's not what you wanted to hear, and I am sorry. I do think our friendship is starting to grow."

Holding her close he closed his eyes. Friendship wasn't what he had in mind, but at least she didn't hate him. For that, he thanked God. Maybe she could learn to love him again. But the ache in his heart was his answer. He was afraid she would never love him again.

Georgie got up and turned over his clothes then she sat back down and snuggled against him again. "I'm sorry I'm so needy. I don't mean to be. I think I've changed that way too. I was a strong, independent woman who could face the world and any problems that came my way. I hope that woman isn't gone forever."

"I don't think she's gone. You've shouldered so many burdens it's time for me to take them off your shoulders for a while. I have a feeling you'll get your confidence back. When your house burned, and you were the only one there for the slaves, that must have been a lot to carry. Heck, surviving the war meant we all did things we didn't want to. If you ever need to talk to me about what happened the day your house burned I'm here. Sometimes talking helps."

She was quiet for so long he thought she'd gone to sleep. But she finally spoke.

"I'm not ready to talk about it now. It does make my heart hurt. Perhaps one day I will tell you the story. It's not pretty, and I had to do a few things I never imagined doing. Let's talk about other things." She offered a weak smile. "I weeded the garden, and I believe we should plant a fall harvest. There is nothing canned in the root cellar. I also need to find fruit to make jam, and jarred meat will be nice for the winter. I do have to say I'm surprised you have nothing hidden away."

"I don't?" He blinked in confusion. "I assumed my mother was taking care of it all."

Shaking her head, she glanced up at him. "I doubt she'd know how. We fine Southern ladies were told to stay out of the kitchen. I only learned how last fall. Since I lived in the cookhouse which we all used, I watched, asked questions and helped. We'll need to find berries for jam too."

"I could have Sondra do it you know."

"Maybe if I run into trouble, I could ask her for help, but I'd like to do it on my own. There is such a special feeling of accomplishment when you do things on your own. I never knew that growing up."

He grinned.

"What?" Her brow furrowed.

"Many women are bemoaning what they'd lost, but not you. I'm proud to have you as my wife. I just hope that one day you'll forgive me for leaving you with Taggart and my mother."

He felt her shiver and tightened his hold on her. "Is it all right to talk about the baby? I mean were you happy about it?"

"Very. I imagined what a child of ours would look like. I came to the conclusion we'd make fine children together. I couldn't wait to tell you. I didn't dare tell your mother or Taggart until one day he went to kick my stomach. I screamed that I was with child and he didn't seem to know if he should continue or stop. I told him to consult your mother before he killed her grandchild." She swallowed hard and then she closed her eyes and shivered.

Helplessness washed over Parker, rendering him speechless.

"Your mother must have told him to be gentler, but he didn't know what that meant. She berated him one day when he was particularly cruel. I just couldn't imagine why you'd trusted Taggart." She gazed at him, sadness reflected in her eyes. "He told me once he saved your life. That answered many of my questions. I concluded that you didn't know how he really was, but then you were gone so very, very long." She sighed and moved away from him. Then she stood and grabbed his clothes, which she tossed to him.

He dressed, slightly amused that she kept her back to him. Then guilt filled him. She wasn't the same woman, and she was right. He was responsible for squashing her spirit. It was always hard to know what to do. Some preferred to be left alone, but if he left her be; he might never get back the woman he loved.

"You can turn around now. What happened to the gun I gave you when we were on the trail?"

"It disappeared." She stared out at the horizon.

He cursed under his breath. More than likely Taggart had made off with it. "I'll get you another one. I wish I could spend more time with you. I've enjoyed my days with you."

She didn't turn and look at him, she just nodded quickly.

"I have a ranch I need to run."

She turned around. "I'll be just fine." She walked to Mine and waited.

He shouldn't have brought up their baby. He lifted her onto the saddle, and then he mounted behind her. He wasn't surprised when she tried to hold her body stiff attempting to keep from touching him, but finally she relaxed and he kissed her head. "We'll get through this. You've got more courage in you than ten men. I do think it'll take a bit of healing, but I want you to know I love you and I'll do anything I can to help make things better."

"I wasn't sure you'd want me now that I'm scarred. I must look hideous."

He reined Mine in to a walk. "They are but battle scars, my love. They'll remind me of just how brave you are, and you don't need to worry, no one but me will see them." His voice sounded husky and he took a deep breath. "You're my wife."

"An unwanted wife."

"An unplanned wife," he corrected softly. "But you are very wanted. Please don't give up on us...or on me. It would break my heart. I now understand why many never want to love again after they lose their spouses or their intendeds. The pain is too unbearable to contemplate."

"I do *want* to love you too," she said with strength added to her words. She was silent for a long while. "I don't know if I know how to love anymore. I feel as though that part of me is broken. I'll be a good wife to you, Parker. We only have three more weeks, and then you can bed me. You'll have to go slow and gently at first. I don't want to end up giving you a black eye." She snuggled against him. "I know that's not what you wanted to hear, and I am sorry. I do think our friendship is starting to grow."

HE LEANED DOWN and kissed her neck. It was a start. He'd get back to building their future, and maybe a routine would help her. He still needed to find a place that would take his mother. One day at a time. He kicked Mine's sides and they galloped home.

THEY MADE it back to the house, but it didn't feel like home to Georgie. In fact, she hated the place. It was full of echoes of her loud screams of pain, torment, and sorrow. It held her heartbreak and the agony of hopes that had been destroyed. But it was where she had to reside.

Parker jumped down and held up his arms to her, and it pained her that she hesitated. Finally, she accepted his assistance, and Parker lifted her down then drew her close to his hard chest. He had given her a bit of time to have fun today and for that, she was grateful. She hadn't been sure she'd ever smile again.

He cupped her cheeks in his hand and kissed her. His masculine lips softened when he placed them against hers.

She sighed and welcomed his tongue as he made the kiss more intimate. He'd heal her heart; it would just take time. They had love between them, she was certain of it. A Bible verse from Second Corinthians sprang to mind.

Finally, brothers, rejoice. Aim for restoration, comfort one another, agree with one another, live in peace; and the God of love and peace will be with you.

Laying her forehead on his chest, she repeated the verse over and over in her mind. She needed to have faith that God would heal her and guide Parker how to help her. An abundant sense of peace filled her and surrounded her. She'd cried out to God many times when she was being beaten, and when it didn't stop, she'd lost her faith.

It was time to let the Lord into her heart and life again. She believed now she would be just fine. Pushing up to her tiptoes, she kissed his cheek. "I'll meet you inside after you take care of Mine." A tugged at her lips, and that brought tears to her eyes.

Parker wiped her tear with his thumb. "It'll be fine."

"I know, that's why I have tears. I believe that God will heal me with your help. I have a feeling that everything will be all right."

He grinned at her. "I'll meet you inside."

She walked to the house full of hope. First thing tomorrow, she was going to pick everything from the garden and then have someone take her to town to get seeds for an autumn planting.

As soon as she walked into the house she heard screaming coming from Millicent's room. Though tempted to go and see what was wrong, she decided she just couldn't. She went into the kitchen to make tea.

Sondra startled and took a step toward the door, her face pasty white. Her blue eyes were wide and there was an expression of fear on her face. All the ingredients to make bread were on the work counter in front of her.

"Sondra, are you all right? What happened?"

"It was my fault. I put a knife on her food tray, not thinking of it as a weapon. As soon as I turned my back to tidy her room, she came at me. I saw her out of the corner of my eye and put my arm up to block her but she got me. I was able to take the knife away from her and I hurried out of there. She's been screaming ever since. I know she broke her china plate and I heard her glass shatter against the wall, I'm assuming." She held a cloth to her forearm.

"Here sit down." Georgie pulled a chair out for her. Then she took the cloth to look at the knife wound. It was deep. "She must have come at you in full force. If you hadn't put your arm up, you could have been killed. I'm going to get some water and see if we can't get your arm to stop bleeding."

"Bleeding?" Parker walked in, took one look and put a pot of water on to boil. "It's going to have to be stitched. Sondra, I'm so sorry. I feel responsible. I knew she could be dangerous but I…" He looked bleakly at his wife. "You did tell me she carried a knife while I was gone. I removed that one from her possession, but I should have known to tell you, Sondra."

"I'm pretty tough. I'll know better in the future."

Georgie blinked hard. "You're going to stay?"

"Truthfully, I don't have a place to go to. This job came at the right time. The other family I worked for was moving farther west, and when I heard you needed someone I was so happy."

"You don't have family nearby?" Georgie asked.

"No, not here in Texas."

Georgie took a wet cloth and put pressure on the wound. "I'm glad you can stay here."

"Thank you. I never thought how hard it would be for a woman to be on her own. With everyone scraping by, folks don't have money to hire help."

Parker nodded his head. "We enjoy having you here. We'll figure out what to do about my mother. It's not safe for her to be here much longer."

"Really, I don't mind."

Georgie stood so Parker could stitch Sondra up. While Sondra had been talking, Georgie had gotten the gash to stop bleeding and Parker had boiled the needle and thread. Though Georgie had never seen anyone boil the thread before.

"Would you like some whiskey?" Georgie asked Sondra. "It can help with the pain."

"As tempting as it sounds, I think I'll be just fine. I'm ready."

Parker's face was grim as he sewed up Sondra's wound. Afterward he bandaged it.

"No more work for you today. I don't want you using that arm." He tied cloth into a sling and gently put it on her.

"I have things I need to take care of. I'll be back in time for supper." He cupped Georgie's shoulders and kissed her cheek before he left.

He looked worried. Too bad she couldn't take his worries away. Why hadn't he gone to his mother; to check on her, at least? Perhaps because the old woman had finally stopped screeching, he'd felt it best to leave her be. A shudder rolled through Georgia as she thought of Millicent and her violent ways.

"I'll make you some tea, Sondra. Would you like to have it in the sitting room or out on the front porch?"

Sondra turned red. "I can't have you wait on me. It's not right. Besides I need to go and clean up all that broken glass and china in Mrs. Eastman's room."

Georgie put her hands on her hips. "You heard Parker, go sit. Enjoy a rest while you can. I don't know if I could stand to watch you get stitched up again."

"If you're sure—"

"Go!" Georgie grinned as Sondra reluctantly left the kitchen.

Georgie cleaned up the kitchen. She'd been the same way when she'd been hurt and things needed to be done. But if she didn't work, she didn't survive. War was never a good thing. She'd heard the Union Army suffered many casualties too. She knew Yankee prisoners of war had been taken somewhere in Texas. A chill went through her. She didn't want to think about any darn Yankees of any rogue Confederates. Too much evil had been done.

It'd been quiet upstairs. Millicent was probably asleep. Grabbing a broom, she went upstairs. The keys to the room were hanging from a peg on the wall near the bedroom door. She took them and put her ear to the door. Not a sound. Still, it would be best to use caution. After she unlocked the door, she slowly opened it. Millicent was lying on her bed with her back facing the door.

Letting out a breath she hadn't realized she'd been holding, Georgie picked up the big pieces of the plate and cup and put them in the hall. Next, she swept the smaller pieces into a pile near the door. Then she took hold of the long handle of the dustpan and swept the mess into it. Millicent didn't move. When Georgia was done, she turned to leave.

"Don't think things are done between you and me," Millicent spit out. "I know you're a fake. You're no O'Rourke from Tennessee."

As fast as she could, Georgia gathered the broom and dustpan and pulled the door closed. She fumbled with the key as her hands shook, but finally the door was locked. Her heart beat so quickly, it made her lightheaded, and she leaned against the wall for a moment. What a fool she'd been to go in there. She bent and picked up the bigger pieces and put them in the dustpan and then went down the stairs. Millicent wanted her dead, and it would be best to remember that fact.

CHAPTER SIX

*S*upper was unusually quiet. He could excuse Sondra because of her pain but usually Georgie had a smile along with conversation. In fact, if he didn't know better, he'd think Georgie was guilty of something. She refused to make eye contact with him. She did ask Sondra if she needed any tending to her injured arm.

Sondra blushed. She didn't seem to like being the center of attention.

"I'm just fine. Give me a day and I'll be back at work."

Parker's lips twitched. He was surrounded by headstrong women who didn't seem to be able to think of themselves first. "I think you'll need more than a day."

Sondra's mouth opened.

Whatever she was going to say, he firmly cut her off. "We'll see how you feel tomorrow night."

"Fair enough, Parker, thank you. Thank you for cleaning all the debris in your mother's room. I would have hated to ask Walter to do it. He's always so busy." She smiled and blushed deeper as she looked down at her plate as though it fascinated her.

"I didn't do it." His eyes narrowed. Georgie had done it, he just knew it. No wonder she was so quiet.

"Georgie, did you get hurt up in my mother's room? You've been awfully quiet tonight."

She glanced up at him and quickly turned her head.

"Georgie?"

She sighed loudly. "Just like a dog with a bone. Yes, it was me. No, it wasn't my finest idea, and yes I will agree to not go in there again." She turned her head and glared at him.

His eyes widened. What had he done? His mother could make even the sweetest turn sour. "Did she try to hurt you? I presume you're not hurt?"

Georgie shook her head. "She was on the bed with her back to me. She did say things aren't done between us. I have to admit I felt a shiver go through me, but that was all."

He grimaced. "Tell you what; let's take a ride into town tomorrow."

Her eyes lit up. "Fort Worth?"

"Fort Worth is a bit far. We actually live closer to Spring Water. I just tell people Fort Worth as a reference. Texas is a big state."

"You'll like it in town, Georgie. Make sure you stop in and have tea at The Kingsman," Sondra told her. "It's a real treat. The owner, Shelly, makes the best pies. Now, don't cause any trouble in there. She's sweet but she can pack a wallop. She planned to take me in, but this job came at the right time. They say that the Lord always provides."

Parker nodded. He wasn't sure he believed much anymore. He'd seen so much suffering during the war. His prayers certainly hadn't been answered.

"That sounds like fun. I'd love to go, Parker!" Georgie enthused.

She reminded him of a small child going to the store for the first time. It felt good to make her happy. He wasn't too excited about seeing the Union Soldiers that had taken over as law in the town. There were a few who were good men, but the others would just as soon spit on a person.

"I want to check with the business owners and make sure they aren't experiencing financial hardships. Those stinking carpetbaggers are like jackals waiting to buy foreclosed properties for the cost of the back taxes. I try to intercede when I can. Those folks in town have worked hard for every penny they have." He paused. The two women stared at him as though they'd never seen him before. "Excuse my language."

Georgie put her hand over her mouth, but laughter came pouring out. "I want to see the stinking carpetbaggers."

Sondra joined in with her own laughter, but all too soon the laughs died down and they looked sad.

"We had carpetbaggers in Tennessee. I know what you're talking about. And as for the Army, you're right there are a few good apples among the bad. It's admirable that you help the town." She gazed at him in such a way he felt ten feet tall.

He captured Sondra's gaze. "I'm going to have Corporal Green do work that is closer to the house. I'd like it if you'd call him to go with you into my mother's room from now on."

Sondra blushed and glanced down at the table. Parker exchanged amused smiles with Georgie. He thought there had been an attraction between Sondra and Green.

"Walter is a good worker. He's kind too." Sondra turned to Georgie. "He's gentle with the animals, and I don't think we'll ever have reason to fear him."

"I'll have to get to know Walter a bit better. I know you both trust him but I think it's going to be a while before I fully trust a man. But I will try." Georgie bit her bottom lip before she stood and started to gather the plates.

"Would anyone like coffee?" Georgie asked.

Sondra started to get up.

"Sit back down, Sondra. You need to rest that arm. Don't worry, I can take care of things while you heal. It's no mark against you if you take some time off."

Tears filled Sondra's eyes. "You both have been so good to me. I don't like shirking my duties."

Georgie took one stack of dishes into the kitchen and she came back out with two cups of coffee. "Here, you two relax while I clean the kitchen."

"You two should be strolling in the moonlight," Sondra said between sniffles.

He took a sip of the hot beverage. "Sondra, drink your coffee. A stroll does sound good though. Georgie, do you need me to help?" He almost laughed at the surprised expression on her face. "I know how."

"I know you know, but most men wouldn't have offered is all. I'll be quick."

He patiently drank his coffee and stood as soon as she came back into the dining room. He held his hand out to her and was more than pleased when she tucked her small hand in his. He led her outside. "Looks like a full moon."

She took a deep breath. "Yes it does. Days certainly get hot here in Texas. I'm glad it grows a bit cooler in the evenings."

He squeezed her hand lightly. "It must have been hard to go into my mother's room. It's not your job to take care of her. I don't want you hurt ever again." He drew her into his arms. She felt soft, and he longed to be with her, but she wasn't ready. He'd been trying to give her space but it grew harder by the day. Plain and simple, he desired his wife.

She leaned in to him and put her ear over his heart. Her arms tightened around his waist, and he stroked her pretty blond hair. She still had places on her back that hadn't completely healed.

"Shall we take that stroll?"

She nodded and stepped back. He offered her his arm and she took it. They walked for a bit toward the pasture where the horses were frolicking together.

He stopped in front of the wooden fencing. "This pasture is where we keep the mares."

"They sure are beautiful. Do you sell horses too?"

"I have a horseman named Crumb, who has a gift for working with horses. He trains them for the hands. When I got home from the war, there were two horses left, and the low number of cattle nearly broke my heart. Both armies had been through and taken almost everything. Crumb hid the livestock in the trees behind the house. If you go in a bit it is thick with foliage, but if you know where you are going you can get through to a circle in the middle of the woods. Crumb built fencing and hid the best livestock we had. He didn't dare hide it all. He didn't want anyone to become suspicious. There wasn't enough room to separate the mares and the one stallion he kept. There were many foals delivered that year. Finally, he cleared some of the thick woods away and built a separate corral for Jefferson. Same with the cattle. He ended up building a separate area for our best bull, Davis."

She laughed and the melodious sound wrapped around his heart. The moonlight enhanced her beauty and his mouth almost became dry as he studied her.

"Is something wrong?" Her voice quavered a bit.

He wanted to swear. Taggart and his mother beat her confidence out of her. It broke a piece of his heart. He cupped her face with his hands and smiled down at her. "No sweetheart, I was admiring just how beautiful you are. I'm grateful to have you in my life and doubly grateful you're my wife." He leaned down and brushed his lips over hers. He stood straight and watched the horses. He didn't want to push her. They had time. It was hard to be patient after all the losses they'd suffered. One day a loved one was there and the next they'd been killed.

"See the paler horse?"

She looked and nodded.

"She's a palomino."

"What's her name?"

"Yours."

She laughed and shook her head. "You really have a knack for naming horses. Mine and Yours?"

"Yes, she's for you."

She looked uncertain and then joy spread across her face. Her eyes misted as she took his hand. "I haven't had my own horse since the first year of the war. My heart was so empty when I first met you, but little by little you are filling it, and I thank you. You can't know what it all means to me." Tears slowly trailed down her face.

"We all lost a considerable amount. I thought I'd forever be bitter, but how can I be when I have you? The smallest of things make you happy. You have the gumption that was so part of the fabric of the South. I don't see it much these days. You make me feel as though I'm ten feet tall when you smile. Much of my family's wealth is gone, and my pride had taken more than one hit." He drew a deep breath. "You make me want to be a better man."

"You make me out to be some type of mystical person. We picked ourselves up and dusted ourselves off. It wasn't easy but it was a necessity. I am glad your mother put the ad in the paper because I have you."

The loud sound of a shotgun blast exploded in the air, and Georgie dove for the hard ground. Covering her head with her hands, she stayed very still. She reacted like some of the soldiers he'd fought with.

Squatting down, he tried to comfort her with encouraging words; whatever came to mind he said it softly. Finally, she removed her hands from her head and peered at him.

"Let's get you up and inside," he coaxed.

She let him help her up and lead her inside the house. He closed the door and she went back and locked it.

"Who is shooting?" Her hands shook.

"Come, sit down." He led her to the sofa and sat down next to her. "We have gray wolves that attack the livestock. Those wolves have become a big problem."

"I want my gun, and you do have a shotgun inside the house, don't you?"

"I think we have enough men protecting the ranch—"

Her eyes grew wide. "I want to be able to protect myself. I'd like a pistol and a shotgun. Oh, and extra ammunition."

"You absolutely certain you know how to use a shotgun?"

Her jaw dropped as she continued to stare at him. "Of course I know how! Who do you think killed all those—" She put her hand over her mouth and shook her head. She took a few deep breaths and then dropped her hand. "Like I said I need to be able to protect myself."

Who had she killed? He shook his head. Now wasn't the time to ask. "Fine, when we get back from town tomorrow you can show me that you know how to load and shoot."

"But—"

"I want to be sure you won't shoot your foot off. If there is a problem, I'll teach you. You're right, it's still dangerous these days."

Her shoulders seem to relax. "I want the root cellar filled with provisions too. It's empty except for a few lamps and oil."

"That's a good idea. Don't worry, we can get anything you need in town. I want you to feel safe here."

She nodded and then was silent, but he could tell her mind was whirling.

Later that night she lay as stiff as a board next to him. He didn't expect anything but maybe putting his arm around her, but he didn't dare.

ANOTHER SLEEPLESS NIGHT BEHIND HER. Georgie stared at herself in the mirror. Where had the carefree girl she used to be gone? So much had happened, and she'd had nightmares once in a while, but ever since the first whip of the crop, she felt different. She'd faced hell before, and it had made her stronger. This time it had the opposite effect, and she didn't like the ninny she'd become.

Was it because she'd thought all her torturous times were behind her once she married Parker? She'd allowed herself to let her guard down, and she couldn't allow that to happen again. She couldn't afford to. Too bad she'd have to wait until they got back from town; she'd have felt better with a gun in her hand. After grimacing in the mirror, she picked up her bonnet from the bed and hurried down the stairs.

Sondra sat on the sofa looking bored while Parker watched Georgie come down the stairs. He smiled at her, and if she'd had one to give back, she would have.

"Are you ready?" he asked.

"Yes. What was the name of the town again?"

"It's called Spring Water. The story is that the original group looking for a place to settle ended up going in circles. One of the men started a fight with the guide by saying 'all you've done is lead us to this same Spring Water.' It stuck." He opened the door for her.

"He mustn't have been a very bright guide. If you follow the movement of the sun you can figure out what direction you're heading. What about the rest of the people in the group? Didn't they notice sooner?"

Parker chuckled. "I guess I never gave it much thought."

She walked outside. "Is it always so hot in Texas?"

"No, not in the winter." Parker lifted her onto the wagon.

She used her handkerchief to dab at the perspiration forming on her brow. Tennessee was hot too. Out of sorts was how she truly felt. Nothing seemed right from her head to her shoes. She looked out at the horizon and immediately felt grateful to God for a good life. Her irritation ebbed. She was just fine compared to many. She even had a dress that was pretty.

"You should put your bonnet on. That sun can be harsh," Parker said as he drove the wagon.

The bonnet was pretty too. It was a light blue with a bit of lace framing it. "Thank you for the clothes you bought for me. I would have felt apprehensive going to town with one of my old dresses." Her heart felt lighter. It was as though God had taken some of her problems and put them on His shoulder.

"There will be a blockade when we get close to Spring Water. They don't allow guns in town. They'll ask why we're there."

"Why would they care?" She shook her head.

"I think the Yankees are nosey." He grinned. "I guess they want to show us who's in charge."

"I avoided going into town back home," she admitted quietly. "Back in Tennessee, I mean. I was harassed too much, and I couldn't stand it. I was lucky to find a neighbor who was taking his family to Independence, Missouri. I just had to help with the chores. His wife was ailing from a broken heart. She lost three sons in the war. There were so many wagons, horses, and people just walking, heading to Independence. I think they all wanted to start over out West. There were too many people who looked half-starved, and I wish I could have given some a ride or food, but it wasn't mine to give. Besides, we had meager supplies as it was."

Turning her head, she saw a look of wonder on Parker's face.

"Don't think I'm saintly or anything," she added quickly. "If it came down to me or them, I'd have picked me. I went hungry plenty of times, and I know it's a bad choice to give your food away."

"You have a good heart, Georgie."

Pretending not to hear him, she pointed to the town. "Oh, it's bigger than I imagined. Tell me what's there."

"The usual. A sheriff's office, a general store, a bank. You'll see."

"Don't forget the Kingsman Restaurant Sondra talked about. Oh, I'm sorry. I don't mean for you to spend money on me. If we could just get supplies for the root cellar, that would be more than enough."

He stopped the wagon in front of the wooden blockade. Three Union Soldiers leaned against the wood with their rifles aimed at Parker and Georgie.

She wanted to get out and run the other way. She'd had more than enough of the war. For some reason she'd thought they'd have less Yankees in Texas. She closed her eyes as her body began to tremble, then she clasped her hands to keep them still. She opened her eyes again and gave the soldiers a faint smile.

One of the men in the blue uniform pushed off from the blockade and walked to her side of the wagon. He boldly looked her up and down.

"Ma'am, I don't think I've ever seen you before."

"She's my wife, Mrs. Eastman."

"I'm Sergeant Hollander, ma'am. I'm in charge. I'm the one who'll be watching you the whole time you're in town;

you and your Reb husband. If you ever need anything don't hesitate to come to me." He tipped his hat.

"We'd like to go into town," Parker said his voice laced with hate.

"Give us your guns," the sergeant demanded.

"Don't have any."

The sergeant narrowed his eyes at Parker. "You're not even equipped to protect your so-called wife."

"She ain't wearin' no ring, Sergeant."

"Corporal MacKen, you were told to keep your mouth shut."

"Yes, Sergeant."

"Private Roberts open the gate. Good day to you, ma'am." Sergeant Hollander tipped his hat to her again while he looked her over again.

It was so hard not to scream. It was even harder to breathe. It seemed to take forever to get through the gate. But finally, Parker reined in the horses and wrapped the lines around the brake.

He turned and took her hands into his. "I shouldn't have brought you here. I should have known how that darned Hollander would act. He gets pleasure by being cruel and trying to bait others. Don't think I didn't want to pound him when he ogled you."

"I'm glad you didn't. I don't want any trouble." She furrowed her brow.

"Not to worry, sweetheart. I don't want any trouble either." He jumped down from the wagon and was quickly at her side with his arms raised to help her to the ground.

What if her trembling wouldn't stop? Slowly she stood and allowed herself to be lifted down. He must have noticed she was still trembling because he pulled close and kissed her temple.

"Be brave."

Nodding she stepped back. She lifted her chin and pulled her shoulders back. She was brave. The first place they stopped was the general store. It wasn't as big as she was used to, but it was well stocked.

"Howdy, Parker!" A tall handsome man greeted.

"Good to see you, Anson. Allow me to introduce my wife, Georgie O'Rourke Eastman, recently from Tennessee. My dear, this is Anson Stack."

The dark-haired, blue-eyed man smiled. "A pleasure to meet you."

"It's nice to make your acquaintance too. Your store looks better stocked than any I've seen in a while. It does a heart good to see it." She smiled at him.

The door opened, and a young, nicely dressed woman entered. Her brown hair was beautifully styled, and Georgie felt a pang of wistfulness. She'd dressed the same way before the war. Georgie nodded her head slowly.

"My, Parker, it must be my lucky day to run into you. I've been waiting for you to speak to my father so we can continue courting. Oh, hello Anson, nice day isn't it?"

"Fanny Chancellor, this is my wife, Georgie O'Rourke Eastman."

Fanny's eyes widened momentarily. "Georgie, that's a male name. What farm do you hale from? I'm a Chancellor of the Atlanta Chancellors. We relocated before the war. I prayed for Parker every day. I was always so worried something would happen to him."

"Yes, I'm acquainted with the Chancellors. One of your relatives had a beautiful Plantation in Tennessee."

"Yes, that would be my father's older brother. I do believe his plantation to be the biggest in that area."

Georgie started to look at items on the shelf.

"It's too bad that area was wiped out. I heard that there is nothing but the poor and the Yanks living there now."

Georgie picked up a jar of jam. "Parker, do you like raspberry?"

"Yes, I do." He gave her an odd look.

She nodded and kept looking and moving farther away from Fanny. Women like that were to be avoided at all costs.

"Everyone knew the Chancellors. Certainly you must have known of my uncle." Fanny started to follow Georgie around like a stray dog.

Georgie finally stopped and turned to Fanny. "I don't know if you told me you're a Chancellor thinking I would bow and scrape to you. But dear, I'm an O'Rourke. I lived in the biggest plantation in the whole state. But really, it's bad manners to make others feel bad. If I wasn't who I am, I would have been insulted but I'll forgive your faux pas."

Georgie walked to the counter. "Mr. Stack, would it be all right if I left a few of these things here? It's hard to shop with my arms full. Next time I will be sure to bring my basket with me."

"Perfectly fine, ma'am."

"Thank you." She put an armload of food items on the counter and walked toward Parker, ignoring Fanny.

"Parker, what else do you suggest we buy? You know I rely on you." She tilted her head and smiled.

His lips twitched. She bit her bottom lip to keep from laughing.

"Well, my dear wife, I think some coffee is in order."

"You are so right. I'll add flour and sugar too."

"Parker, what am I to tell my father?" Fanny asked while forming her lips into a pout.

"About what?" His voice was very casual.

"We had an understanding."

"Fanny, I do believe it was my brother you wished to marry. It's not up to me to take his place. Besides, I found a wonderful woman to be my wife. We're very happy together.

If your father would like a word with me, I'd be more than happy to talk with him."

Fanny's jaw dropped. She closed it and practically ran out of the store.

"I feel bad for her," Georgie said. "What she thinks important just isn't anymore."

Parker put his arm around her shoulders. "You handled her beautifully. In fact, I would have treated her with a hint of real meanness."

"I wouldn't have said anything at all, but she wouldn't stop trying to belittle me. I guess I won't be invited to attend any quilting parties."

"Does it matter so much?" Parker escorted her to the counter.

"Not at all. I'm just like everyone else. Besides I've been very busy being a wife." Heat flooded her face at the implication of what she had said.

"Anson, could you wrap this all up for us while we visit the Kingsman? I'll pay you when we're finished."

Anson smiled and nodded. "Sure thing, enjoy the Kingsman."

They stepped outside onto the wooden walkway.

"I forgot something," Parker said. "Be right back." He hurried back inside the store.

GEORGIE GLANCED AROUND THE TOWN. There was a bank across the street right next to the sheriff's office which was full of soldiers. Farther down, she saw a saloon and a livery. There was even a place to have clothes washed. It probably did a booming business with the Yankees in town. The Kingsman was right next to the general store. There were other wooden buildings, but they mostly appeared to be empty.

A sign in one of the windows across the way read *Reopening Soon*. Had Parker had a hand in saving that business? She knew him to be kind but he was much kinder than she knew.

Parker returned to her side, and as they left the store, he offered her his arm. It cheered her as they walked even if it was only to the establishment next door. He opened the door for her and she liked the inside right away. The tables were covered in blue gingham with red gingham napkins. None of the chairs matched, and pieces of art hung all around.

"Parker Eastman," A tall woman with her brown hair braided down her back and pretty blue eyes said as she hurried over to them. "I heard you up and married." She sighed. "And here I am pining away for you." She placed her hand over her heart and winked at Georgie.

Georgie offered a polite smile.

The woman stuck her hand out. "It's a pleasure to meet you, Mrs. Eastman. It's about time this old cowboy got himself a wife. I'm Shelly Kingston."

Georgie shook Shelly's hand. "Call me Georgie. It's nice to meet you."

"I've got a table in front of the window if you like. It's a nice view if you don't look at the soldiers." She chuckled as she led them to the table. She waited as Parker held out the chair for Georgie and then seated himself. "Menu is on the board. I'll send some coffee over unless Georgie you'd prefer tea."

"Sondra recommended the tea."

A wide grin spread across Shelly's face. "I'm so glad she landed on her feet. She's been a good friend to me. Tell her I said hello."

"We will," Parker said.

Shelly turned and walked toward the kitchen.

Georgie spread her napkin over her lap and looked around some more. "The pictures are amazing. Do you think they're of local places?"

"They are. A girl named Natalie paints them. Her father is a mean old cuss and doesn't like her wasting her time on what he considers trash. She paints when he's not around and gives the pictures to Shelly. They're for sale. Natalie is hoping to make enough to get away from her dad."

Georgie frowned. "That's sad. She's very talented." Too bad she didn't have the funds to buy one of the pictures. "I never asked if we could afford all the items we bought. I just put things on the counter with no consideration."

He leaned forward and put his hand over hers, and tiny tingles of excitement shot up her arm. "It's fine. We have more than enough."

"Oh, good. I don't want you to think I'm frivolous with money."

Shelly returned placing their beverages onto the table. "What'll it be?"

Georgie spoke first. "I would like the steak with potatoes, please."

Shelly turned her attention to Parker.

"I'll have the same."

"That's easy enough. It'll be ready soon." Shelly went to the door to greet more customers.

Georgie peered out the window. "She's right about the soldiers. There sure are plenty of them."

"See the blond one standing in front of the sheriff's door?"

She nodded.

"That is Major Cooke. He's the only honest one in the bunch. If you ever need help, ask for him and make it seem as though you know him personally. Some of the soldiers have no sense of decency."

"It's the same on both sides," she admitted with a trace of sadness. "We had enough of our soldiers pillage our supplies, and then there were the bushwhackers. If I hadn't hidden, I hate to imagine what they would have done. They ruined a neighbor's daughter. At least they didn't kill her. When it happened, though, she wished she was dead. But survival was the important thing."

"Was it bushwhackers that burned your house?"

She shook her head. "No, it was the Yankee Soldiers." She frowned. It wasn't a time for sadness. "I bet the food is good."

"It is. Plus Shelly could use the business. Not as many come to town to eat since the occupation."

"I wanted to ask about the building down the street. It has a sign that says it will reopen. Was that your doing?"

He nodded. "It's a dress shop. There haven't been many people buying new dresses lately. I suggested she make cheaper, ready-made clothes. The clothes you have were made by her."

Georgie fingered the hem on her dress sleeve. "She is a fine dressmaker. But I think you were right when you said not many can afford new dresses."

"She's also teaching quilt making classes and the like. Apparently, making clothes and quilts were not what many Southern women were taught."

She smiled. "You're right about that. I can't sew a straight line. I did make clothes from the fabric we had at the house. The first dress I made, one sleeve was much longer than the other and the hem was crooked. I could benefit from her classes."

Shelly made a beeline for them and set their plates in front of them. The smell was heavenly, and it made Georgie's mouth water.

"Thank you, Shelly."

"My pleasure. Enjoy your meal." Shelly was off again waiting on other customers.

"She doesn't have waitresses?" Georgie cut a piece of steak and popped it into her mouth. "Oh, my. I haven't had steak in so very long." Closing her eyes as she chewed, she savored the juicy meat.

"I've been remiss. You can see cattle from the house. I'll be sure you get your steaks."

Deep warmth spread through her. His tone had been one of sweetness, and he didn't say it as though he expected something in return. If only she wasn't so afraid of his touch. He'd always been gentle with her, and he seemed to enjoy their nights together when he held her as much as she had.

They finished and said goodbye to Shelly with promises to be back soon. Upon their return to the wagon, they found it was filled with their purchases.

Georgie sighed. "I suppose it's time for us to go home."

Parker gazed at her. "Do you truly think of it as *home?*" He looked so hopeful.

"Most of the time," she acknowledged with a weak smile. "I still have my moments when I want to run free through the pastures and the woods and be far away from it. But I never want to run from you." Without knowing what else to say, she stared down at her feet.

The next thing she knew she'd been lifted up and placed on the wagon seat. Their gazes collided and his was intense.

"It's a start." He went to the driver's side and climbed in. Once again, they were stopped before they could leave.

"I hope you don't get ambushed with you not having any guns on you." Corporal MacKen sneered. The other four soldiers laughed and opened the barricade.

Georgie held on to Parker's arm until they passed through. "Did I hurt you? I was holding on too tight." She looked over her shoulder expecting to see the soldiers coming after them.

Parker slowed the wagon and leaned over to kiss her cheek. "You do have quite the grip, but I'm fine."

"I don't understand why you'd take a chance and travel unarmed?" She furrowed her brow.

Parker held the reins in one hand and with the other opened a hidden compartment under the seat. It held three rifles and two guns. He grinned at her.

She sat there stunned as she stared at the weapons. "I assume they're loaded?"

"They sure are." For a moment, his eyes glinting with amusement. Then he grew serious. "I would never take protecting you for granted. Not ever again. Do those soldiers really think we'd go into a blocked off town without our guns? I know there are a few towns that used to do it because there were too many men getting drunk and shooting up the place but it was the sheriff, not soldiers, that made that rule. Most wagons around here have compartments. If you're riding a horse you drop off your gun behind…" He swept his gaze around the area. "Well, see that big boulder over there? Then we collect them when we leave. I wouldn't trust them to give me my gun back."

He drove past the huge rock and stopped. He grabbed his gun and gun belt from under the seat and strapped it on. "If anyone's compartment is found, there will be a big X on this rock, warning the rest of us. You never know if the Yankees are in a hanging mood or not."

Her heart beat faster as she realized the danger they'd been in. "What if they'd found your guns today?"

Parker shrugged. "I'd just say I just bought this wagon and didn't know about the secret place to stash guns."

The knuckles on her hands turn white as she clasped her hands so hard. Would they always have to live in fear? If only there hadn't been a war. She remembered how proud the women had been when Father and Daniel had joined up for the cause. No one expected the hardships that happened.

"You've been home for about two years year haven't you?"

"About that." He gave her a sidelong glance.

"Why aren't you married? It seems as though there are single women in town."

He was silent for so long, she thought he wasn't going to answer her.

"The girl who promised to wait for me married someone else. I had no idea until I got back to Texas. She'd been writing to me the whole time. She spoke of love and a family with me. I don't understand such deceit. I didn't want to marry and have to pretend to love another." He didn't look at her he just kept driving.

Pretend to love? There were times she wished she'd never answered the mail order ad and this was one of them. She'd hoped that once she worked out her fears they'd be able to have a good marriage with love and laughter and children. But if he was only *pretending* to love her, then how could that be? It would just be a façade. She took in a slow deep breath and slowly let it out trying to calm herself. It wasn't his fault; his mother had arranged the marriage. She'd known it was a chance she had taken, coming to Texas. Her eyes burned while she watched the countryside. There was nothing she could change. If he was only pretending, she'd just have to accept a loveless marriage.

If only she'd never asked the question. The house came into sight, and relief washed over her. She'd need to find some time alone to lick her wounds. She almost laughed. Ever since she'd been at the ranch, it had been one wound after another.

He reined in the horses and tied off the lines before jumping down. When he got to her side, she tried to smile but failed. She didn't make eye contact with him. They had a lifetime together and it wouldn't do if they couldn't get along. Her heart squeezed painfully as he lifted her down and held her waist a bit longer than usual.

"If you'll excuse me I'm not feeling well. I'm going to go lie down." She hurried inside and up the stairs. Millicent was screaming and Georgie thought she might go crazy herself if she had to listen to that woman much longer. After walking into the room she shared with Parker, she closed the door and the tears came. She'd survived so much. Her family was all dead, she had fought off soldiers and worked extremely hard so the people she felt responsible for were fed. She'd managed the hardship of a wagon train and survived cruelties carried out by Millicent and Taggart. She'd even lost her baby. She had never completely broken, but now she felt destroyed.

She had wanted to be able to lie with Parker and have children. She'd been trying to work out her fear, but now it didn't seem to matter. Who was the woman he loved? She was probably a pretty, biddable wife who wouldn't have been any trouble. It didn't matter, though, did it? It was too soon yet to try for another child. She had a strong backbone, but she needed to rest, both her mind and her body.

She sobbed for a bit and then just lay there, spent, clutching a pillow against her chest. She needed to get up and make supper, but she had no will to leave the room. The door opened. It had to be Parker. She hugged the pillow harder. She hadn't a clue as to what to say to him.

The bed dipped as he lay down. He spooned her, wrapping his arm around her waist. She was too much of a mess to protest.

"Sweetheart, I heard you crying. I wasn't sure if I should have come to you then or wait. I'm here now. Tell me what's wrong." He kissed her temple and pulled her closer to him.

"I'm just so tired. I want things to be the way they were before the war. I want to feel safe. I know it sounds frivolous, but I want to go to a party and be courted. I want to fall in love, and I want a family."

He stiffened behind her.

CHAPTER SEVEN

The next morning, Parker watched Georgie make breakfast. He knew her to be capable, but her apparent skill amazed him. She had the coffee made before he was up and then helped Sondra get dressed. Georgie settled Sondra on a chair in the sitting room and brought her a cup of coffee.

She finally stopped long enough to say good morning to him. "Do you need more coffee?"

He smiled at her. "I'm fine. How's Sondra?"

"Discouraged her arm isn't better by now. It's only been a little over a day." She shrugged her shoulders and smiled. "She'll have to be patient, but I know how it feels. Pancakes and bacon good for you?"

"Sounds wonderful. I'm glad you snuck off to the kitchen when you were a child. I'm reaping the benefits." He enjoyed the sway of her hips as she stirred the thick batter.

"Seems like a lifetime ago. Every skill I learned or had to learn has helped me to get to this place in my life. I sometimes wonder if the simpering belles I knew died of starvation, though I did hear some married Union Soldiers."

He furrowed his brow. "I never thought about it. You could have saved yourself a lot of traveling if you'd done the same."

Her eyes flashed at him in anger when she turned around. She crossed her arms and stared at him as though she'd never seen him before. "I suppose if I wanted to be as low as those Yankee snakes. I lost so much to them, I'd rather die than marry one." She uncrossed her arms and sighed. "I suppose you do what you have to, to survive. I'm just different is all. Now I wonder if the belles' parents made them marry?" She grew quiet and turned toward the cook stove.

When he did catch a glimpse of her face as she cooked, she looked to be brooding. "I have to ride out to the northern pasture today. I won't be home until near dark."

"I'll be sure you have a hot meal when you get home," she replied without turning around.

Maybe one day she'd say something about missing him all day, but for now, it was apparent she didn't feel that way about him. He had thought her feelings for him to be deeper, and it had shaken him last night to discover they weren't. How did a man court his own wife?

"Here you go." She set a plate piled high with pancakes in front of him. Next, she put the bacon on the table. "I'm going to help Sondra."

He watched her take a plate with only two pancakes and some bacon on it out to the other room. Maybe he'd ask a few of the married men what they did to court a woman. Flowers of course, but there must have been more.

There was a knock, and the kitchen door opened. Corporal Green entered and took off his hat. "Good morning, Captain. I thought I'd take Mrs. Eastman's breakfast up to her and then check on Sondra. That is, if it's fine with you."

"It's perfectly fine."

Georgie joined them carrying an empty plate. "Good morning, Walter. I'll just be a minute fixing a tray for Millie. Why don't you go on into the other room and visit with Sondra. Maybe you can convince her she needs to rest her arm."

Walter smiled. "Thank you, I will." They watched him leave.

"You call my mother Millie?"

"Just behind her back." Georgie's eyes sparkled as she smiled. "I know it's not right, but it makes me feel so much better. I don't know why exactly. I'll stop."

"No, don't stop if it makes you happy."

She laughed and the sound of it warmed his heart. "You're beautiful."

Her face grew red. "Would you like more coffee?"

Compliments went on his courting list. "I wish I had more time to spend with you today, but I do have a lot work I need to get to."

"Don't worry about me. I'll be fine."

He couldn't read her. Was she really fine with him being away? Was she worried? He stood and closed the distance between them. Now he could read her. She tensed her body but he still put his arms around her and pulled her close. It was a very strange feeling since she was so stiff. He bent and kissed her cheek. "I'll miss you." He kissed her cheek again.

After letting go, he gave her a grin, and his heart lurched when she smiled back.

"I'll miss you too." She said it so shyly, and it made his whole morning.

He lifted his hat off its peg and went out the front door. He didn't even bother saying good bye to Corporal Green and Sondra. He just repeated Georgie's *I'll miss you too* in his mind over and over until he got to the barn. He stopped suddenly and his eyes grew wide. He knew he cared for her but when had her happiness become his? He'd best proceed nice and slow so he didn't get his heart trampled on again.

Mine nickered as Parker came near. "At least someone is happy to see me." He patted the horse's neck. "Let me get you saddled, and then we have work to do. "You know, Mine, a man ought to know better than to get involved with a woman. They turn you in circles and your heart inside out. They make it so you don't know if you're coming or going and what you thought was right is wrong."

Parker finished saddling then mounted up and began to ride to the north pasture. Now, where would he find flowers?

Corporal Walter Green marched up the stairs with Millicent's tray. A short while later, a loud crash came from the second floor. Sondra and Georgie stared at each other. Then the door slammed, and the sound of it being locked seemed louder than usual.

Walter sprinted down the stairs with a crooked smile on his face. "Pancakes aren't her favorite. She was up and dressed. I'll go up in an hour or so to get the tray back."

Sondra took a step forward and touched his arm. "Did you get hurt?"

Georgie bit back a smile. Love was blooming on the ranch. Then her smile faded. Why couldn't that be her and Parker?

"I think you might want to send for more plates. She broke another one." Walter chuckled.

"It might be a good idea to get tin plates for her," Georgie commented.

"That china is probably priceless," Sondra bemoaned.

"It isn't expensive china. I'd hate to lose more though." Georgie lifted a big straw hat down off the peg and set in upon her head. "I'll be out gardening for a bit before the heat sets in." She took a small spade and a basket off the shelf and headed out the back door.

Gardening gave her much time to think. Part of her was more than grateful for the life she was living. The selfish part of her wanted Parker to love her. It had been a blow to learn that he didn't despite him having told her he did. Sometimes she was so stupid. He had gotten past her guard. It seemed a man either loved someone or he didn't. They'd been together long enough for him to know.

A terrible tightness lodged in her throat. He was her strength, and it was wrong. Her confidence had waned. She'd been proud of the way she'd held soldiers off in Tennessee, but that didn't mean anything to her now. She wasn't brave, and she certainly wasn't the woman who had met Parker for the first time. She was capable and could do anything she set her mind to, but she now questioned her every decision multiple times.

Parker had called her beautiful, but did he mean it? Maybe he thought it was something husbands said to their wives. She wasn't the pretty one, her sister, Amy, had been the pretty one. That's probably why she was killed first. Amy had gone to town the day before the attack and Georgie often wondered if Amy hadn't attracted one of the soldier's interests.

A rare cold breeze hit her and she shivered. Standing she peered all around but she didn't see anyone. It felt as though she was being watched. After shaking her head at her foolishness she picked up all her garden supplies and the vegetables she'd picked.

She made enough noise coming in just in case Walter and Sondra were having a private moment but they were just sitting at the table talking. "It looks like we'll have a good supper." Georgie held up her basket of vegetables."

Sondra grinned. "You have a way with plants. All I saw when I first looked at the garden was a patch of weeds."

"Would anyone like more coffee?" Georgie held up the pot. They both declined, so she poured herself a cup and sat at the table with the couple. She traced the rim of her cup with her finger. Finally, she just had to know.

"Do you know the woman Parker thought was waiting for him so they could marry?"

Walter shifted in his chair. "So he told you about her. It near broke his heart. It was mean spirited of her to play with Parker's affections like she did. Even after she married another, she wrote to Parker declaring her love. It was a slap in the face when he rode to her home and was told by her mother that she had married almost a year ago."

Sondra nodded. "They'd been promised for a year before the war. He wanted to get married before he left, but she refused. Why she'd marry a man who faked an injury to get out of service is beyond me. Rose Mc, er Callen now, did Parker wrong. If you marry another, then you tell the truth. Poor Parker thought he had a sweetheart waiting for him. I heard it was an awful blow to him. We didn't see much of him. People said he'd thrown himself into making the ranch a success. Besides losing Rose, he lost his father and brother. He'd known about his brother, but finding out his father was dead too was a shock."

"You two certainly know more than I had thought." Was it town gossip or was it the truth?

Sondra gave her a weak smile. "His mother told everyone she could find. It was as though she wanted sympathy for his tragedy. We'd already treated her gently when her son and husband died. She is one for attention, and she didn't spare the details in her storytelling."

"Where is Rose now?" Georgie stared down at her coffee almost afraid of the answer. If Parker's former intended lived close, they might never be able to have a good marriage. Parker still loved Rose.

"Her and her husband lived on his ranch, but after Parker came back, her husband sold the land, packed them up, and moved them farther west. I'll never forget how Parker looked. He'd been so thin when he came home, but after the news of Rose, he was a shadow of the man he used to be. But he grew stronger, and the ranch prospered." Sondra reached across the table and squeezed Georgie's hand. "He seems content to be your husband."

Surprised, Georgie glanced up. "Does he really? I'm just not sure. I don't know if he has any love left for me. Things might have been different if our child had survived. A child might have brought us closer." It hurt to swallow, and her eyes burned with tears. "I didn't mean to lay my problems at your feet." She turned her head away from them, shamed that she wasn't loveable.

Walter cleared his throat. "Sondra, would you like to take a walk?"

"Yes, fresh air might do me good. Will you be all right if we take a walk, Georgie?"

"It sounds like a fine idea," she managed to say. She only needed to hold on for a few minutes more, and then she could break down. Listening for the door to open and then shut, she finally sighed in relief.

Poor Parker, it must have been devastating when he came home. It was time to stop feeling sorry for herself and start seeing things from her husband's perspective. He probably didn't fully trust women or their love. What a shame. He must have truly loved Rose, and perhaps he still did. A body could be mad at someone and still have intense feelings for that person.

Somehow, she'd have to allow herself to get closer to him. She tilted her head back, hoping to stop the tears. After everything she'd lived through and then Taggart, she just couldn't find it within her to be affectionate. It felt more like torture to allow anyone to touch her.

It wasn't a matter of trust. She trusted Parker, but she still shied away from intimacy. What if she became pregnant again? Was she strong enough to bear the grief if the next baby died too? How was she to buck up and be the wife she wanted to be; the wife she'd been before…?

She pushed the chair back and went to the counter. She might as well get the vegetables chopped. She'd make one big potful of hearty stew with plenty to put into jars and set up in the root cellar. What had they done the previous winter? Maybe they'd used all of the canned food.

She couldn't figure out a way to let go of her fear. Once upon a time laughter and hugs had filled her days. How would she find her way back to the girl she had been then?

She tried to put those troublesome thoughts from her mind as she readied the ingredients for supper. She'd be able to plant for a fall harvest soon. Pretty quick, the stew was bubbling on the stove, and she wiped her brow as she stood back and glanced around the kitchen, proud of all she had accomplished.

Sitting outside appealed to her. Hopefully a cool breeze would come by. After pouring herself some water she went out front and sat in a chair. The light wind was anything but cool but it was better than sitting inside. What a view! The live oaks swayed as though they danced to an unheard song. The long grass waved, and the sunflowers were an explosion of color. It was easy to see why Parker's father had chosen this spot to build a house. According to Parker, he owned all the land farther than her eyes could see. It was obvious he held a deep love for the land, and he worked hard.

Her own father had been an idle man who really didn't like to work. You would have never found a callous on his hands. Actually now that she was thinking about it her mother was the same way. Why work when you had slaves to do it. She shuddered. Of course she supported the South but she never supported owning people and treating them like pack mules. Hopefully, they had all found their way to a new life.

Now that she thought about it, she hadn't seen one Negro person when Parker had taken her to town. And yet, Texas had been a slave state. How utterly strange. She'd have to ask Parker about it.

Out of the corner of her eye, she caught a flash of dark blue near the barn. Her heart pounded, but fear didn't stop her one bit. She immediately ran into the house and grabbed a rifle and ammunition. Frantically, she looked through the windows to see where Sondra and Walter were. She had to warn them in some way. But how? Where were they?

Was there one Yankee out there? Or more? She rushed up the steps and opened Parker's chest. She immediately saw what she was looking for. As quick as a wink she rushed to the window and hung the confederate flag out of it. She closed the window on it to keep it in place.

Next, she raced down the stairs and put two pistols in her apron pocket and loaded the rest of the rifles. Then she put a rifle by each window. Now where was he? She stared at the barn and saw him creeping along the side of it. He stilled as he gazed at the flag. He actually smiled and started toward the house.

Was he trying to die? After locking the front door, she crawled beneath the windows and took up a rifle. She aimed at the ground in front of the Union Soldier. Dirt kicked up when the bullet hit. When he looked up she recognized Private Andrews.

"I've got you surrounded. Come on out and we can talk a while," he shouted his lies.

She hadn't had time to lock the back door. She'd have to go with her gut that the Yankee was alone. She aimed the rifle and shot at his feet.

He swore, and his face hardened. "If I have to drag you out of the house I will! Did you know I could have you hanged for flying that vile, useless flag? Which will it be Mrs. Eastman, a bit of fun or stringing you up?"

How much trouble would she be in if she killed him? Would maiming him be a hanging offense? This time she aimed and shot his hat right off his head.

"Who ya got in there with you? Ain't no way a woman can shoot like that." He took another step forward.

Her mouth went dry, but she kept her hands steady. She aimed, but before she could shoot, someone else shot him right through the heart. He went down hard.

"I got him! I got myself a miserable viper of a Yankee!" The yelling was coming from Millicent's room! How had she gotten a gun?

Georgie kept her focus on the front of the house. If there was one Yankee there might be more. She didn't see anyone, so she crawled to the back, locked the door, and studied the area. No movement could be detected. It was back to the front for her.

She breathed heavily as her heart pounded. She'd wait until dark to go get the body. Meanwhile she'd keep guard. She wasn't going to let a Union Soldier take her down. She'd fought too long and hard.

Someone was frantically knocking on the back door. She slowly made her way to it and quietly unlocked it and scrambled back, her rifle aimed and her pistol lying on the floor next to her. She held her breath as the heavy wooden door slowly opened. Her body tensed as she got ready to shoot.

"Georgie it's us. It's Walter and Sondra."

"Hurry in and then lock the door! I don't know if there are more of them out there."

Walter took one of the rifles left at the back window. "What happened?"

"That Yankee wanted me to come out and play with him. He did mention stringing me up if I didn't. We need to keep watch. Here, Sondra take the pistol just in case."

Sondra paled but picked up the gun.

The sound of horse hooves pounding the ground put Georgie on high alert. Quickly, she crawled to the front and took aim. Maybe with Walter and Sondra she could hold them off. And there was Millicent.

Parker led the big group of men. They had their guns drawn as they rode around the barn and house. Parker jumped down and ran to the front door. Georgie unlocked it and then took her post at the window.

"Georgie!"

"I'm here, Parker. Get down before you get your head blown off."

He sat down and gently pried the rifle out of her hands. "It's safe now. My men are outside and they are trained gunmen."

Walter walked into the front room.

"Walter, go get the flag down."

Georgie grabbed Parker's arm. "No. Your mother has a rifle. She put the Yankee down."

"Sondra, stay with Georgie. Walter, come with me. We'll need to check what my mother is doing. How'd she get a rifle?" Parker asked.

"I was wondering the same thing. Be careful." Georgie started to tremble. Try as she might, she couldn't stop the shaking.

She sat on the floor with Sondra holding her hand while the men climbed the stairs. The sound of the flag being taken from the window came first and then the sound of Millicent's door opening. Georgie held her breath.

"I got me one, Parker! I got a yellow-bellied Yankee. Didn't he know the war is over? Your wife is a good shot. Put a hole in his hat but she wasn't about to kill him. So, I did."

Georgie put her hand over her mouth. What were they going to do now?

Walter came back down the steps while Parker murmured something to his mother. Walter's eyes gleamed as he smiled at Georgie. "If we had you as a soldier we might have won." He took off his hat and raked his fingers through his hair.

She didn't answer, she was waiting for Parker. Finally, the door upstairs closed and Parker walked down the steps.

He locked his gaze on Georgie, and when he reached her he squatted in front of her. "Are you hurt?"

"No," she said breathlessly.

He helped her to stand and held her in the circle of his arms. Her body still trembled.

"He wanted, he wanted to, I know he planned…" Tears stung her eyes.

"Walter, tell the men to bury the body far from here and to let his horse loose in a different direction. Then I want them to ride over all tracks leading from town to here."

"Right away," Walter replied crisply, and then he left.

"Is there anything I can do?" Sondra asked. She was now seated on the sofa.

"Do you think you can gather all the rifles and guns? I know your arm is hurt."

"Parker, it'll be fine." Sondra touched her hand to her heart for a moment before she went toward the kitchen.

Georgie lifted her head and stared into Parker's eyes. "I would have killed him if he got to the porch. I shot the dirt in front of him, but he wasn't deterred. Not even when I shot his hat off. Then the next thing I knew he was shot dead, and I didn't do it."

He pulled her closer until she laid her head against his hard chest. His heartbeat calmed her, and she eventually stopped trembling. She pulled away and sat on the sofa. Parker sat on a chair next to her.

"Hanging the flag was a fine idea. We heard the shots, and when we approached, we saw the flag and knew what we were looking for. You placed a rifle at each window? A clever move."

Worry still gnawed at her. "I loaded them all so I could swiftly shoot if needed. I saw blue and I watched and I saw blue again at the barn. Walter and Sondra were taking a walk, and I didn't know how many Yankees there were." It was as though an emotional dam opened, and her words poured out. "I expected more than one. I guess he didn't think I was a threat, he kept coming closer and closer. He said he had the house surrounded but I already checked and I didn't see a speck of blue out there. Did you know hanging the flag was a hanging offense? He said he wanted to either have some fun with me or string me up. I know what his type of fun includes, and I wasn't about to allow myself to be at his mercy." Her skin crawled.

"It was Andrews," he said in a tight voice.

She nodded. "I recognized him."

He had so much anger in his eyes, she expected him to explode at any time. He gripped the arm of the chair. "I should have been here to protect you."

As his voice got louder, Georgie cringed. "I think I did just fine by myself. These are senseless times we live in. I'm strong and capable. I've seen the worst life has to offer, and I won't allow it to be that way again." She reached out and held his hand. "Now tell me how Millicent had a rifle in her room."

He entwined their fingers. "My heart is beating so fast. I could have lost you." He took a shuddering breath. "Apparently, she had the key and took one of the guns you put by the upstairs window. She has no love for the Union Army. She is very proud of herself and you."

Georgie studied his face and could tell by the lines on it, he was worried. "The rest of them are going to come aren't they?" Bile filled her stomach.

"I don't know. The best thing to do is get you as far away from here as possible. I'm just not sure where yet. I have friends in the Arizona Territory, but I don't know how safe it is to travel there." He frowned as he momentarily closed his eyes.

She stilled at his words, and she wanted to go and hide. There was no reason to send her away. Letting go of his hand, she winced and turned her body away from him. It was easy enough for him to make the decision to have her leave. His words shocked her. Hadn't she proven that she could handle herself? "I'm not leaving. I'm safer here with you."

"Don't you understand? I can't always be here. I need to get you to a place where they won't be looking for you."

She couldn't look at him, and she decided not to say a word. He might think he was sending her away, but he was wrong, so very wrong.

CHAPTER EIGHT

*P*arker glanced at his wife as he drank his morning coffee. It had been a long sleepless night. Georgie had tossed and turned; her nightmares were back. She allowed him to comfort her for about ten minutes before she returned to her side of the bed, lying as stiff as a board. He doubted she ever went back to sleep.

She'd hardly said more than a few words to him. He didn't like the way her shoulders slumped or the dark circles under her eyes. The sooner he got her out of here the better. Maybe if she changed her name she could hide out in one of the bigger towns in Texas.

Before long, she placed a plate of eggs and bacon in front of him. She didn't even look at him. Just fixed herself a plate and sat down across from him, but she didn't eat.

"Not hungry?" He tried to make his voice soothing.

It was almost as though she didn't hear him. Finally, she gave him a false smile and then rubbed the back of her neck before standing and looking out each of the windows.

"This is the exact reason you need to leave. You're as nervous a cat near water. It'll be best for everyone."

She faced him but looked off to the left of him, scowling. She crossed her arms and stalked into the sitting room.

Groaning, he left the table and followed her. It was for her own good. Why couldn't she understand? He walked up behind her and cupped her shoulders in his hands. She was shaking all over.

"Don't touch me. You want to be rid of me, so as far as I'm concerned we're not even friends." She flinched and rolled her shoulders until he dropped his hands.

"What are you talking about?"

She turned, and the sorrow on her face surprised him. "There isn't anything to talk about. You're my husband and of course I'm supposed to blindly do your bidding, but I can't. Things have changed so much since the closeness we had driving the wagon here. I thought we suited each other. I thought you had an understanding of me and what I'd gone through. You admired my strength and know how but none of it matters anymore. I'm disposable. Did Rose suddenly become a widow? Is that why you want me gone?"

He would have felt better if she cried instead of her eyes looking like she was dead inside. "I haven't heard a word about Rose."

"I see. Well there are enough empty-headed females in town that would be more to your liking and they aren't damaged inside. I don't really blame you fully for wanting to send me away. I've done things in Tennessee that no woman should have had to. I lost your baby, and now I don't like to be touched. Not what I'd call a good wife. I came here with practically nothing but the clothes on my back. You had to go to great expense because of me. Even your mother is locked up due to my presence." She took a shuddering breath. "I'll go but on my own terms. I can take care of myself. I'll decide where I'll move on to."

He widened his eyes. "What? You most certainly will not go anywhere until I find a place for you."

She stared at him with her dead eyes again saying nothing. She then whirled about and walked up the stairs; probably to have a good cry because that was what she had been doing lately. He scowled as he watched her go.

There was no way to make her understand, and he had work to do. Why wouldn't she just listen to him and do as she was told? He slapped his hat on his head and walked out the door, slamming it closed. He'd find somewhere for her to go and she would go.

She found a carpetbag and began to fill it with her things. She hesitated briefly, wondering whether to include the clothing he had purchased for her. But then she decided she should. After all that had gone on at the hands of his mother, surely she deserved what had been given her. She carried the carpetbag down the stairs and found Parker's saddlebags, which she filled with supplies. Next, she went into his hardly used office. She needed to find some type of map. After rifling around in his desk drawers, she found some. She'd head north and then west to meet up with the Southwest Trail. She would wait for a wagon train to come along and join them. She could go all the way to California if she wanted. Carefully, she folded the map and put it in the saddlebag.

There were bedrolls in the barn. If she could saddle her horse without anyone knowing, she'd be able to get away. Her heart ached. She'd been many things, but stupid hadn't been one of them until she had come here. Since her arrival, she had seen more violence and heartbreak than she could have ever imagined.

Sondra and Walter went to pick berries for jam, so if she was going, it had to be now. Taking a deep breath, she grabbed a coat and hat along with the saddlebags and carpetbag and walked to the barn.

Her palomino nickered when she approached. Georgie patted her neck. As quietly as she could, she saddled Yours and loaded her things on. Then she led her mare outside to a big rock. Getting on top of the rock was the only way for Georgie to get on the horse's back. Once seated, she slowly rode away without looking back. There was nothing for her there. Her future was ahead of her.

The Union Army patrolling the road had not been part of her plan. She saw them from a great distance and rode into the woods, where she stayed very still and quiet until they had passed. They were probably on their way to the ranch. A sigh slipped out. Now she couldn't go back.

She continued going north pulling off the road when she saw anyone. She wasn't going very fast so she only stopped once to water Yours. She now hated that name since it was part of his horse's name, Mine. Her stomach felt queasy, and a sense of dread filled her. It was because she'd never see Parker again, she told herself.

The sky grew dark. Rain clouds rolled in quickly, and the drop in temperature made Georgie shiver. She quickly put on her coat and buttoned it up and then looked for a place to hole up. All she saw were trees or prairie. The trees would have to do.

As fast as she could, she unloaded Yours and then led the horse to a grassy area and picketed her. Turning in a circle she tried to determine where would be the best place to wait out the rain. She decided on a grouping of trees that grew close together creating a canopy of leaves. She ate the bread and cheese she'd brought and unrolled her bedroll. Too bad she hadn't thought to pack a rain slicker.

It started to drizzle, and Georgie went to Yours, took her reins and led her under the canopy, making it just in time. Minutes later a deluge of rain fell, and she wasn't as proud of herself as she sat drenched on a saturated bedroll. What she had in the saddle bags was probably fine but she didn't hold any hope that the carpetbag kept the water out.

Georgie took a deep breath and released it, seeking calm. It was just uncomfortable, and the rain would stop at any minute, she mused. Texas rain was like no other. The sheer amount that came down made her jaw drop. The next thing she knew she was sitting in a puddle. It was raining faster than the earth could absorb it. She stood up and put the bedroll over a branch to allow the rain to wash the mud out of it.

It got colder the later it got. Soon it would be night, and she'd have no fire. Good thing she had a rifle and pistol with her. She might need them tonight if animals decided to make a meal of her or Yours. Still, she didn't regret leaving. There was no way she was going to allow Parker to tuck her away somewhere so he could forget her.

She'd thought he was everything a hero was made of, but he was a hero who didn't love her. Her bitterness wouldn't leave, but maybe it wasn't his fault that he couldn't love her. He'd never wanted a wife, and if he had his choice, certainly he would have never picked her. The easiest thing would be to say she was a widow, but she wasn't sure if she could live that lie. It would depend on her options.

Her body shook as she became chilled. It had been a long night staying awake. She expected to see wolves, but perhaps they knew where to hole up and stay dry. At least the rain had stopped, and the sun was on the horizon. She quickly ate some bread and loaded up to continue her journey.

Miserable would be the right word. Yes, she was miserably wet and she didn't feel as though she was getting any dryer as they rode in the sunshine. Again, she was able to find a stream. She dared to open her carpet bag and found, though things were damp, they weren't as soaked as what she was wearing. Stopping early to lay her things out to dry would be a wise move.

Parker was probably livid when he had found her gone. She hadn't thought about how worried Sondra and Walter would be either. It couldn't have been helped, though.

She gazed into the distance. Tomorrow she'd turn west.

PARKER THREW his hat on the ground. How could she have left? How? Where was she going? Stubborn woman who didn't know what was for her own good! Had she even survived the storm last night?

To top it off, a few soldiers had been at the house yesterday looking for Private Andrews. Walter had answered their questions, but they'd promised to come back when the land owner returned. Walter told him they weren't happy. Here he was sitting on the porch with his rifle across his lap while he drank coffee. Georgie really made the best coffee he'd ever had, but he never told her. Why had he not said anything?

He'd known she would balk at being sent away, but he never thought she would leave on her own. It was a gutsy, yet incredibly stupid move. Didn't she know of the dangers? Depending on which direction she went, she was bound to be captured by either the Apache or the Comanche.

He had sent two of his soldiers, Sandler and Willis, after her, but that had been hours ago. He looked up at the sky. Oh, God he'd be so grateful if she came back unharmed.

Motion caught his eye. His little talk with God was being interrupted by the sight of the Union Army bearing down on him. Maxwell, Green, and his foreman Cabot were in the house with rifles ready.

Parker was relieved to see Major Cooke leading his troops. He was at least a fair enough man compared to Sergeant Hollander. Parker remained seated as though he hadn't a care in the world.

"Good Day, Eastman," Major Cooke said, reining in his horse a little too close to the porch. "We are looking for Private Andrews, and we have reason to believe he was here."

"Why would he come here? Was there a message you wanted to get to me? I don't usually see you unless you need some cattle or you've come to claim the taxes." He shot Cooke a pointed stare. "By the way, I still haven't been paid for the cattle I sold you. I'm in no position to give them away." He picked up his cup and calmly drank from it. The calmer he remained, the more riled they would become. This wasn't his first go round with these men.

"If I see him I'll tell him to get back to town before he's considered a deserter. Is there anything else I can do for you?"

"We'd like to search the premises and talk to your wife."

Parker stood up and spread his legs shoulder width. "Now what business do you think you have with my wife?"

Major Cooke had the good grace to turn red. "He saw your wife in town and had taken a fancy to her. He said he was coming here."

Parker made certain to keep his rifle pointed down as he took a step forward. "To do what?"

"I'm sure I'm not privy to the sergeant's thoughts."

Parker eyed Sergeant Hollander. "I bet you know why he came."

"Just tell us where he is, you mangy cur rebel," the sergeant spit out.

Parker gave him a blank stare. It made the sergeant look bad.

The major cleared his throat. "May I please speak to your wife?"

"I told your men yesterday she left. Ranch life wasn't for her. She's a Southern Belle from Tennessee. She wanted to go home." He didn't miss a beat; he'd been lying to Yankees for years now.

The major narrowed his eyes. "Just how was she to get there?"

"Three of my most trusted men are escorting her. I believe they were going to go east then north." He sat back down as though he hadn't a care in the world.

"He's lying!" the sergeant shouted.

"Sergeant get a hold of yourself! Now Mr. Eastman, we both know the Comanche are in a great number in the east." The major looked impatient.

"One of the men is a Comanche. They'll have safe passage."

The major smirked. "This is not a slave state anymore. I could take you in."

Parker cocked his left brow. "I doubt anyone would be able to keep a Comanche as a slave. All my men would have been killed the first day. He likes being a cowboy, and he has a way with horses. Don't worry he was raised in a good Christian household. They found him when he was a baby left in the woods. So you see he is not a slave." He shrugged. "Look around if you want but make it quick I have cattle to tend to. My mother is in a locked room. She has become a bit of a danger. She's not in her right mind, so please leave her door shut." He heard the back door close. The extra people in the house were gone. He stepped aside and gestured for them to go on in.

Sondra rounded the corner of the house. She put her hand to her throat. "Mr. Eastman what is going on?"

"Sondra come sit with me. The soldiers want to search the house." Parker had to keep his lips from twitching.

"We don't have bootleg whiskey if that's what you're looking for," she snidely told the major before she sat down next to Parker. He took her hand, and she gazed at him with adoration.

The major stared at the two of them and shook his head. "No wonder she left," he murmured.

"Did you say something, Major?" Parker asked, faking a look of concern.

"Sergeant Ricks and Corporal Buyers you're with me." The two men hurried to join the major inside.

"You know this will be all over town faster than a wild fire," Sondra said.

"I know and thank you. It's just as well she's not here. I might have taken matters into my own hands if they'd interrogated her. But I'm worried about her. She could be dead by now."

Sondra patted his shoulder. "I have a good feeling she'll be back. Why, she loves you. I don't think she even knows she does, but it's right there for the rest of us to see by the way she looks at you."

His jaw almost dropped. "That can't be right. I let her down. And the beatings she received from Taggart and my mother buried the love she might have felt for me. She doesn't like for me to touch her most of the time. I really don't know what to do. I loved the woman she was before all this happened."

She tilted her head. "You don't love her now? I thought marriage was for better or worse."

"She left me. It's as if she yanked my heart out." He

grimaced. "I think we should talk about this after our company has gone."

Sondra began to nod when they heard screeching.

"I told them not to open her door!" Parker jumped to his feet and started for the door.

"Hold it right there, Reb. No one goes in," Sergeant Hollander commanded as he cocked his pistol.

Parker stopped, turned, and scowled at the other man. Then a shot was fired, and Parker felt as though his heart had jumped into his throat.

"I don't care if you shoot me. That's my mother in there!" Parker ran inside.

Corporal Byers came down the steps carrying Millicent.

For a moment, Parker thought maybe she was still alive, but there was so much blood.

"I-I'm...s-sorry," said the young corporal.

"Give her to me!" Parker took his mother into his arms and buried his face in her hair. How could she be dead? His body trembled, and when he lifted his head, he glared at Major Cooke.

"Out! Get out of my house this instant, and I want whoever shot her in jail. I told you not to open that door. It was locked! You murdered my mother while looking for your deserter. Get off my land and may you rot in hell, all of you."

"I apologize—"

He narrowed his eyes into a glare. "Major, I said get out!"

The Union Soldiers hurried outside. Moments later, the sound of departing hoof beats came from outside.

Parker knocked a few cups off the dining table and laid his mother upon it. He stared at her with tears in his eyes, and his throat felt as though it was going to close up.

"Parker?" Sondra called. She walked into the dining room and screamed.

Walter, Maxwell, and Cabot all raced inside, and as soon as they saw the body, they removed their hats and bowed their heads.

"You want us to go after those Yankees, Captain?" Sandler asked.

"No, we'll get our revenge one day. For now, I want all men to be on their guard. I don't trust those yellowbellied cowards. I told them not to open her door."

"I'll let the rest know, Captain," Sandler saluted him before he left.

Sondra had gone upstairs and returned with a bedsheet that she placed over his mother. He thought he might be sick. He'd lost his whole family to the Union Army. He had no illusions the soldier who murdered would be punished. Watching Walter comfort Sondra, he felt bereft. How he wished Georgie was there.

He should have kept her by his side and gently wooed her like he'd planned.

GEORGIE SQUINTED up at the sun. Had she gone too far north before turning west? Where was the Southwest Trail? It was heavily wooded where she'd pulled up, and she didn't remember so many trees before. She wiped the perspiration off her brow with her sleeve. Her handkerchief was filthy already. She was lost. How could that have happened?

She released a heavy sigh and allowed her shoulders to slump. She had the map, but without precise landmarks it had been hard to judge where to turn. She must have missed it. She leaned back against a tree and drank some water when she heard a twig snap. Someone was out there.

As quietly as she could she moved Yours behind a thicket and watched. She put the water away and held onto her rifle.

A man wandered into sight. His clothing was more tattered than her worst had been, and it looked like he had never in his life trimmed his beard. She put her hand over her mouth. He bent to look at something, then, muttering, stood again, dropping the dull gray metal trap he had just inspected.

She stroked Yours to keep her quiet. Now she'd have to be on the lookout for traps. The burly man didn't look friendly, and she wished he'd move along. It had been stupid to run away, but it was a fine time to realize it now. Would she be able to find her way home? Probably not. She'd end up traveling all of the big state of Texas and never catch another glimpse of Parker.

The trapper looked around as though he knew he was being watched. His beady eye narrowed as he sniffed the air. He walked deeper into the forest, but she didn't move for a very long time. Her gut feeling was that he was lying in wait. Her patience saved her. He finally stood and glanced around again. This time he just shrugged and walked away.

Her heart pounded so hard. She led Yours out of that particular stand of woods but kept a wary eye out. She'd go south in case she had missed the turn off. Exhaustion filled her from her lack of sleep as she found a well-worn path and turned south. She climbed into the saddle and off they went. Her gaze darted from left to right to left again. There were too many creatures in these woods, including the trapper.

Her heart had been shattered by Parker and it might not ever be whole again. If she couldn't find the Southwest Trail, she was out of luck. Why she had thought it would be easy she hadn't a clue. But at least she still had enough food and there had been plenty of creeks. Yours was a good traveling companion. She'd been well trained.

What was Parker doing right now? He was her only family, well there was also his mother, though Georgie preferred not to think of her as family. It was too late now;

he wouldn't want her back. He didn't respect her and that tore her in half. They'd had such a beautiful budding love, or so she'd thought, but any hope for their marriage had been destroyed. Somewhere along the trail, she'd determined that she *could* pretend to be a widow because she'd never want any other man but Parker.

If she could have been more normal, maybe he wouldn't have wanted to send her away. She hadn't killed the soldier, his mother had, but he hadn't mentioned sending *her* away. Was he just using it as an excuse to be rid of her? It was done now, of course. She'd taken the decision out of his hands by leaving, so the why didn't really matter, but she couldn't stop thinking about him.

She didn't even know what love was anymore. She thought for a time that he did love her but it was all pretend. Her belief that she loved him might have been wrong too but her heart was shattered. If only Mama was still alive, she'd be able to sort things out so Georgie would understand her jumbled, contradictory feelings. Someday she'd heal from all she'd been through.

This time she was on the right path. She came to a fork in the road. This must be where she'd gone wrong. She recognized the path she'd traveled and considered her options. One way took her back to Parker and the other to the Southwest Trail. After reining in Yours, she studied each path. The pain in her heart was excruciating as she turned toward the Southwest Trail. She'd have to stop soon and wash her clothes on the bank of a creek. No one would allow her to join their wagon looking as she did. Maybe she could find a place that didn't talk of war.

She rode on for a few hours before she found a fast flowing creek. She could wash there. She unsaddled Yours and let her wander between the creek and the grass. The mare never once tried to leave her.

She took her dirty clothes out of the carpetbag and shook her head. She wouldn't get them pristine, but they'd be clean. She took the pile of clothes and a bar of soap and then strode to the creek. She sat and took off her shoes and stockings. She'd need to pound the clothes against some rocks to break up the dirt. It was going to be hard work but it wasn't anything she hadn't done before. She found it to be easier to be standing in the water if the water wasn't too cold.

She wet the first shift, laid it on a big rock, and scrubbed it with soap. Luckily, no rock pounding was needed. She then rinsed it, wrung the water out of it and threw it onto a patch of grass. She'd lay it out to dry when she was done.

There weren't many clothes, but the ones from the rain were covered in mud. There would have been a time she'd have thrown the clothes away but those times were gone. She scrubbed her dress against the rock. She got some of the mud off but there were numerous stains on it. First, she sighed loudly but after the sigh, she just did her best. On a wagon train, people wore clothes that had become stained and frayed along the way.

Horses' hooves echoed, and she raced out of the creek then she dove for her rifle and hid behind a tree. A chill ran down her spine. She took a calming breath. She'd either live or die that day, and there was no help for it. Yours' ears twitched, and she returned a nicker from another horse.

Peeking from behind the tree, Georgie almost cried in relief. It was Parker's men, Sandler and Willis. She stepped out from her hiding place and narrowed her eyes as she stared them down.

Willis tipped his hat. "Ma'am. Captain Eastman ordered us to find you and bring you home."

She set the rifle against the tree within reach. "So what you are really saying is Parker is ordering me home."

Willis rubbed the back of his neck and glanced at Sandler. "Ma'am, we just have our orders."

"Well, you might as well give your horses a rest. I'm washing clothes."

Sandler glanced down at her bare feet and his turned a bright red. He dismounted and seemed to be at a loss at what to say. He turned to Willis, who just shrugged.

She pretended they weren't there and walked back into the creek. Finally, she felt bad for them. They looked decidedly uncomfortable. "I planned to stop here for the night. My clothes still have to dry. Feel free to make camp."

By the time she finished washing and laying out the clothes, the men had a fire going and a small tent set up. Coffee was set near the fire, and from the smell it was just about done. Willis was slicing up a big piece of ham, and Sandler was making cornbread. She'd go back with them. She didn't want them to be fired.

But it wasn't because she secretly wanted to go home. No, sir.

"Did that husband of mine say why he wanted me?" She put her hands on her hips and narrowed her eyes.

Sandler tipped his hat back. "He said something about you getting lost."

"He also has a concern for your safety. There are plenty of Comanche, Yankees, and the like swarming Texas." Willis took the pot of coffee off the fire. "Would you like some?"

"Yes. I'll get my cup." Was Parker being highhanded or was he really concerned for her safety? She found her cup in her saddlebag and handed it to Willis. She could imagine her sister wanting to flirt with the shy blond.

"Are you all right ma'am?" Willis asked as he handed her cup back to her.

"Yes, why do you ask?"

"You sighed rather loudly."

Sandler's lips twitched. "Willis, you never mention noises a woman makes."

Willis' head tilted and his brow furrowed. "Really? I never remember my mama teaching me that." He sipped his coffee. "In fact, I know she never mentioned it."

Sandler sat down on a fallen log. "That's because she knew not to mention it." Sandler laughed so hard he almost doubled over.

She tried to keep a straight face, but the laughter was infectious and soon she joined in. Willis frowned for a moment before he too laughed.

Georgie sat next to Sandler on the log as Willis took a spot on the ground. It had felt so good to laugh. When was the last time she laughed or smiled even? "So we return to the ranch tomorrow?"

Sandler nodded. "The sooner we get you home the better for everyone. The captain can be a bear when he's mad. It shouldn't take more than two days."

"Two days? It took me forever to get here, and when Parker drove the wagon it took almost a week."

"We know the shortcuts. We got here in a day and a half. Maybe you got lost." Willis turned the ham steaks over.

"Yes, I ended up in some really dense woods. I saw a trapper, but I hid well enough."

Sandler stood with his rifle as did Willis. They slowly turned searching the area. They looked again and moved to different places scanning the area again.

"When did you see the trapper?" Sandler asked never taking his eyes off their surroundings.

"A couple hours at least. It might have been longer. Why?"

"No reason. I was just wondering."

"Ma'am, can you check on the ham?"

"And the cornbread?"

What in the world was going on? "I'd be happy to." The

ham she pulled off the fire but when she checked the cornbread it wasn't quite done, and she left it cooking.

"He's dangerous?" She inquired as she took up her rifle. All she got from the two men was silence. That was answer enough. She took the cornbread and let it cool. Suddenly their little camp was eerie.

Sandler walked backward toward her. "I'm sorry, but we can't wait for your clothes to dry. We need to get out of here as soon as possible. He probably plans to come back for you later after he's done checking all his traps."

"You think he was already here?"

"Yes, I do. We'll leave the tent, a few items of your clothes, and the fire burning as we make our escape. If he checks on you, he'll think you're in the tent. It'll buy us time. Pack what you need to take and stand guard while I saddle the horses and pack whatever else we need."

She hurried to her clothes and left her chemise and pantalets. What woman would leave those behind? After shoving her cup in the saddlebag and her wet dress and cloak into her carpet bag, she carried them near Yours.

"I'm set." She held her rifle and scanned the tall grass and woods nearby. In no time at all Sandler brought her horse to her and helped her mount. He and Willis both mounted in one clean movement.

"Follow me," Willis whispered.

Her nerves were taut and she was going crazy at the slow pace Willis was setting. He was doing the right thing, but everything inside her screamed run. They went in a completely different direction. Sandler rode behind her, and she felt guilty for putting them in such a position.

After an hour, Willis stopped, held up his hand, and turned his horse into the woods. He didn't stop until he found a spot with enough cover for all three of them. He dismounted and quickly helped her off her horse. "Grab your rifle," he whispered.

Fear combined with her frayed nerves was a lot to overcome. She sat with her back against the massive boulder they were behind concentrating on all the sounds. The Wilsons had taught her how to listen to her surroundings so she'd know if something changed.

The birds in the woods across the road became silent, and then suddenly they rapidly flew away causing her to flinch. Her body began to quiver, and it took all her inner strength to be still. Her firm grip on her rifle turned her knuckles white. She stood ready for battle.

"Get behind us," Sandler whispered.

Georgie took a step back. Willis and Sandler exuded complete confidence as they watched. There was silence again and it frightened her. She'd rather see the danger than know it was coming.

A bear of a man wearing worn buckskins waved his arm over his head. "Howdy! I know you're there. I lost my horse, and I've been without food for a few days now."

Her stomach clenched. "That's him."

"We know." Willis' voice was so soft she hardly heard him.

The trapper approached very slowly smiling as he walked. "I'm so hungry. Perhaps you have some hardtack? I won't be no trouble."

Sandler ducked down, pulling her along with him. He put his finger to his nose, and she bit her lip.

"I ain't got nothin' neither. No vittles, no sir. I'm just a poor man trying to find his family. Lost them in the war, I did." Willis barely showed his head, just enough to watch the trapper.

"Well, I'm not all that hungry after all. I'll just take the woman and go. I'll even let you live." His voice sounded closer.

Sandler crawled to the farthest end of the boulder and slowly raised his head.

Georgie's heart pounded. What if both men got shot? She put her hand over her mouth to keep quiet.

"You and the girl might as well come on out. Is she your wife? Are you pleased with her?"

Willis stood straighter. "She's my sister. He cocked his rifle and aimed it. "I'm telling you to leave."

"You best put that away. You might hurt yourself. You ain't never been a soldier." It sounded as though the trapper was trying to goad Willis.

"Don't make no never mind. I can shoot. In fact—" Willis ducked as a knife flew where his head had been. As it dropped, Georgie's eyes widened. It was right next to her.

"Missed, did I? Well I'll be going now."

Willis put his hat on the end of his rifle and raised it. Two quick shots came from nearby. She needed to run, but Willis grabbed her and held her.

"Got him!" Sandler kept his rifle trained in the direction of the trapper as he walked out from behind their hiding place.

"Yep, he's dead all right."

Willis let go of her and she ran out to see it with her own eyes. Her breathing was labored as if she'd just run for an hour.

Sandler unwrapped her whitened fingers from her rifle. "It's fine. Why don't you go stand yonder with the horses? Willis and I are going to drag the body behind the rock. Hopefully, no one will be looking for him."

Willis stood next to her. "He's a big one. Why do we always end up dragging the big ones?"

She gasped.

Willis gave her a contrite frown. "Sorry, ma'am."

"I understand, and call me Georgie. I never did like

ma'am." She tilted her head to them both before going to the horses. It wasn't long before they joined her. Sandler helped her up onto Yours and handed her the rifle.

"We'll be making tracks from here on out. We need to get you back home and out of danger. Be sure to tell us if you're too tired to go on."

"Thank you, Sandler." She was already too tired to go on, being emotionally spent. Sandler was right, though; they needed to be far away from this place in case someone else came. These days, people shot first and asked questions later. She fell into line behind Willis.

As they rode, she tried to put the whole incident out of her mind, but it was near impossible. They stopped once for a quick rest and some stale biscuits. What a shame they'd had to leave most of their food at the false campsite. Now it was almost night, but they still continued. It grew darker and darker but as soon as the full moon appeared, they had more than enough light to keep on.

Her back and legs and her backside all hurt tremendously. But she'd continue all night and into the morning.

Willis dropped back to ride at her side. "Georgie, we can either stop now or continue on. It's two more hours at the most. Sandler and I are used riding like this, but I know you're not. Frankly I'm surprised you've made it this far."

"I wouldn't have but for being on a wagon train. Long days of walking. If I got off Yours now, I'll never be able to get back on. Let's continue and get it over with.

CHAPTER NINE

*P*arker raced off the porch and ran toward his wife. As he got closer, her pallor and weariness concerned him.

"What happened?" he asked Willis.

They reined in the horses. "That trapper we tangled with once a few weeks back caught sight of your wife and planned to have her. Don't worry, he won't be bothering anyone again. We decided to get as far away as possible. We rode part of the day yesterday, thought the night, and kept ridin' until we got here."

"Didn't you take Mrs. Eastman into consideration?" Parker demanded.

"Parker," Georgie interrupted. "They asked me several times if I wanted to stop, and I did not. It was my decision. They saved me from a fate worse than death. Willis and Sandler are heroes. I'm so tired, but if I try to get off my horse my legs won't hold me."

Noting the pleading in her eyes, he immediately whisked her off the horse and into his arms. He kissed her cheek.

"Welcome home." Without another word, he turned and carried her into the house and up to their bedroom.

When he set her on the bed, she cried out in pain.

"Saddle sore are you?" He couldn't help his curtness.

Tears spilled from her eyes and down her cheeks, leaving streaks on her dusty face. "I'm sorry."

Sorry for what? Leaving? Disobeying him? Breaking his heart? He stared at her.

"If you could ask Sondra to help me into my nightgown, I'd appreciate it." She didn't look at him. She kept her gaze on her hands, which she kept wringing.

"Don't move. I'll return in a minute."

He went down the stairs and put water on to heat. Georgie needed to relax her muscles in warm water. Part of him was relieved, and part of him was livid. He wanted to pamper her and hold her but he also wanted to walk away from her.

Finally, he thanked God she was back. Then he grabbed the tub and carried it up the stairs and into her old room. He lit a fire and found a towel and a female bar of soap his mother had loved.

When he was finished, he stood at the doorway watching her. She had her hands over her face. Her body jerked as she sobbed. She gazed at him for a moment and then tried to get up. She ended up plopping back down on the bed.

"I know you really don't want me here. I heard you getting my old room ready."

He'd never seen her so sad. "No, what you heard was me setting up the tub and lighting a warm fire for you." He went to his window and opened it. Leaning out he yelled to his men. "I need hot water brought upstairs and poured into the tub." He pulled himself back in and closed the window.

"Here let's roll you onto your side. It'll feel better while the bath is getting ready."

"I'm sorry to be so much trouble. Really I am." She wasn't strong enough to be of any help moving.

He couldn't help but smile at her tenderly. "You've been through a lot and you're exhausted. We'll talk about it in the morning. For now just let me take care of you."

"But Sondra—" Her voice was so low.

"You'll need to be lifted into the tub. I'll help you. Let's get these clothes off of you."

Her body went still, and she frowned.

"Do you honestly think I'd take advantage of you after all you've been through? I'm not some type of monster who has no consideration for his wife. I know you feel vulnerable, and I'm nervous I'll touch you and you'll think it wrong. Right now almost anywhere I touch you is going to be a pit painful. Sitting in the tub will help your muscles relax. Then I'll put some horse liniment on you."

Her mouth formed an O while her nose wrinkled.

He chuckled and heard one of his men yell the bath was ready. "It's time. Let's get you undressed. I'll be a gentleman."

His gaze met hers, and she studied him as though trying to read his mind. She must have been satisfied with what she saw. She bobbed her head up and down slowly.

He sat her up and unbuttoned the front of her dress. He tried not to brush his fingers over her skin, but it was impossible not to. It was a good sign that she didn't flinch or shy away from him. She just looked so sad. He framed her face with his hands and gave her a tender kiss on her lips. When he drew away, her smile was wobbly and tears were in her eyes. Parker finished getting her undressed. He'd handed her a sheet so she could cover herself as he exposed her skin.

"Whew! That's done. I'm going to lift you. Cry out if you have to."

She didn't say anything, but she bit her lip.

He took a deep breath and lifted her into his arms as

gently as he could. She immediately wrapped her arms around his neck, probably to take some of her weight off his arms so it would hurt less. Surprisingly she didn't cry out as he made the short walk to her room.

Gently and slowly, he set her down into the steaming water. Her sign of relief eased him. He hated hurting her.

"You aren't mad at Willis and Sandler for riding that long are you? It seemed quite necessary at the time. They did ask me if I wanted to stop, but I knew I wouldn't be able to sit a horse again once I got off. They saved me. You have very smart and brave men." She lowered her eyelids as she sank down into the water.

"I trust them with my life. That's why I sent them after you. How'd you end up in that trapper's part of the woods?"

Opening her eyes, she grimaced. "I got a bit lost. I don't know who makes your maps, but they are near impossible to follow. I must have made a wrong turn and when I didn't recognize anything, I decided to head west. The woods got denser, and I hid when I spotted the trapper." She sighed again. "This bath feels so good. He didn't act as though he saw me. I watched him leave and waited a while before going on my way. I finally found the right road and was washing my clothes when your men found me."

"I take it the trapper saw you and followed you."

She gave a weak nod. "He apparently was waiting for nightfall. My heart is in my throat when I think about what could have happened. Is your mother sleeping already? I haven't heard her scream the whole time I've been back."

For a moment, the words wouldn't come. He swallowed over his emotions. "She was shot by the Union Army. They insisted on searching the house for any sign of Private Andrews. I told them not to open the door to her room and the next thing I knew, she was shot, murdered." He didn't try to hide the bitterness he felt. "We buried her today."

"This is my fault. I should have been here." She covered her face with her hands.

"No, it wasn't your fault. In fact, at the time I was relieved you weren't here. They insisted that Andrews had come to see you and never returned. They would have taken you in for interrogation, and I don't think I could have let them without killing a few of those Yankees."

She made small splashes as she dropped her hands back into the water. "I'm so sorry, Parker. It's always so hard to lose a part of your family. She was the only family you had left."

He handed her the fancy soap, enjoying her smile as she held it to her nose and sniffed. "I do have family, I have you." He watched for her reaction and was pleased when her smile grew wider. It felt wonderful when his shoulders relaxed. He was still upset she had left on her own, but now wasn't the time to bring it up.

"I'm sorry I wasn't here to help bury her." She handed the soap back to him. Maybe giving her Millicent's soap wasn't such a good idea. Now Georgie would smell like his mother.

"Ready to get out?"

"Yes." She bit her bottom lip again before he even touched her.

Gently, he helped her stand up, wrapped her in a towel, and then carefully lifted her up into his arms. When he got to his room, he unwrapped the towel and laid her down on her stomach. How odd, the scent of the soap on her skin was not the same as it had been on his mother. He was thankful.

"I have to warn you. This ointment smells pretty bad. I'm used to it, so don't worry about me."

She turned her head in his direction. "How bad can it be?" He opened the jar and she began to cough. "That is powerful smelling. Are you sure you're supposed to use it on people?"

It started as a deep rumble and the next thing he knew he

was laughing. It was a great loud, long laugh. It pushed aside any lingering resentment he had toward her.

"Yes, my love, it's for people too. I could ask one of them men to stand outside of the door and confirm it."

"Now I know for sure you are just being silly." The laughter in her voice did him good.

Rubbing the liniment on her proved to him he wasn't a saint. Even knowing she was in pain he couldn't help but feel aroused by her. He'd never try to send her away again. She squirmed beneath his hands. "I know it has a warmth to it, but I swear you'll be a bit better tomorrow."

"I can tell by your voice that you're enjoying this."

"It's not every day I get to see your adorable backside. I'm a mere man, and of course I'm enjoying the view."

"Lecher."

Parker grinned at her lighthearted accusation.

"There, all done. I'm going to drape a sheet over you. I want you to sleep."

"Thank you, Parker. I wasn't sure you'd want me back. I am so sorry about your mother."

He bent and kissed her cheek. "Thank you, and of course I wanted you back home where you belong."

Her deep, even breathing told him she was asleep before he left.

He ambled down the stairs and into the parlor to find Willis and Sandler waiting for him. They stood as he walked into the room.

"Get some sleep. You two deserve it. Georgie told me what happened. You can fill me in another time. Thank you for bringing her back to me."

"Yes, sir!" Willis said.

Parker gave them a single nod. "See you tomorrow."

He watched them leave and then practically collapsed onto a chair.

Sondra hustled into the room with a cup of coffee. "Try to relax. She's back."

"Thank you for the coffee. I'm planning to tell her you're unavailable. Otherwise, she'd demand you tend to her, and I want to do for her. I need to build a closeness between us again."

"I understand. Get some rest. I'll be in the kitchen."

His prayers had been answered, and Georgie was safe and in his bed. He rubbed the back of his stiff neck and savored his coffee.

"Don't you have ranch things to attend to?" Georgie had spent enough time with Parker the last few days. Besides, he made her stay in bed. If he left for a bit, she could get up.

"No, I don't. My main concern is you, love."

She glared at him.

He widened his eyes. "What's that look for?"

"You always call me love or my love and it hurts to hear you say it." Her heart felt heavy.

Parker sat on the side of the bed. He took her hand into his. "You still don't believe that I love you?"

"I don't know. The look on your face when you told me about the woman you love, Rose Callen, said it all. You still pine for her. It took me completely by surprise since I thought you did love me. I've been hurt and angry ever since. I always wanted to have a husband who loved me. I know I was forced on you, but I could have sworn that you returned my feelings. You *said* you did."

He put his hand under her chin and lifted it then gazed into her eyes. "The only thing I feel for Rose is bitterness and betrayal. If she couldn't have remained faithful to me then she wouldn't have been a good wife to me. All she had to do was tell me in a letter. She still talked about us getting married up to the end. I didn't think I'd ever be willing to try to love another."

His words put a fire in her soul, but he still didn't say he loved her.

She moved over and patted the empty space on the bed. When he sat next to her, she was pleased. "I suppose it's my turn to tell you why I have nightmares." She started wringing her hands and finally placed them on either side of her.

"We lived on one of the biggest plantations, and yes I was a spoiled girl when the war started. I hadn't even had a coming out party yet, and my sister cried due to the lack of suitors. My brother Daniel signed up right away. He was so very proud and we were too, but I was afraid he'd never come back. My father refused and when they came for him, he sent a slave in his place. I've never said it, but my father was a coward. He inherited his wealth and never really worked a day in his life." She took one of Parker's hands and traced his callouses.

"His hands were as soft as mine. We heard later the slave he sent ran away. I was secretly happy, but my father was livid and he went raging down to the slave quarters. I never did find out what he did but there came the sound of the whip and so much wailing. I tried to go down the next day to see if anyone needed medical attention, but I was forbidden." She closed her eyes trying to get the sounds of the wails out of her head.

"The first time the Union Army came my father meekly handed them supplies, and he took to his bed for the rest of the day. It was the first time I'd heard my mother criticize my father. My sister, Amy had batted her eyelashes at the soldiers and gave them coy smiles. She made me so mad. Anyway, I took it upon myself to hide both food and live-stock in the woods. The overseer, Bently, helped me. We decided to leave enough in the house so if they came back there was something for them to take, but I also hid all the silver and a lot of the jewelry. When some of the slaves saw what I was doing they came and helped me."

She took a deep breath. "The next time the Union Army came, my father decided to shoot at them. He was a foolish man. I was near the side of the house and I quickly lay down behind some bushes. I remember the sun was starting to go down. They stormed the house and dragged my father, my sister, and my mother outside. I had to keep my hands over my mouth to keep from screaming. Everything within me wanted to run and help them."

"That would have been foolish," Parker commented as he took her hand in his.

"They just shot my father then they, they did things to my sister and mother. I could barely see due to all my tears. Their screams were terrifying and then they were silent. I could hear the soldiers talking and wondering what happened to the other sister. I'd never been so scared in my life. They took everything left in the house and then threw torches inside. It was amazing just how fast the house burned down." Tears began to fall, but she swiped them away.

"They rode out as quickly as they rode in. I stayed where I was until Bently found me. I ran to my father first and took the gun he had in his waistband. I didn't like the way Bently looked at me, and he knew where all of the valuables were. They slaves came running but they didn't dare tangle with Bently." Could she tell him this last part?

"He tore my clothes off right there in front of everyone. He touched me... everywhere. I threw up and he backhanded me, and I fell onto the pile of my clothes and grabbed the gun. He'd just undone his breeches and was coming for me when I shot him dead."

Sobbing, she couldn't help but shake. She could smell the

sulfur from the gun mixed in with the smoke-filled air. There was complete silence afterward, and the next thing she knew she was covered with a man's shirt.

"Is that when you made the cookhouse your home?"

His question jarred her out of her musing. "Yes, with the help of all the people on our land. I immediately freed them but I didn't have any paper give them, papers proving their freedom at the time. Eventually I was able to do it for them all. A few left, but most stayed. They hid me every time either army stopped by.

"But no matter which side came they thought the women were theirs to have. I have the blood of both Union and Confederate men on my hands. I wasn't going to allow it. I armed everyone on the plantation and soon enough we were left alone until the war was over. I think they came to me first demanding money for taxes. I was surprised there wasn't a price on my head.

An oh-so-kind neighbor insisted they work the crop so he could take it. We'd planned to sell it out from under him, but we weren't clever enough and he got to it first."

"One of the freedmen heard that there was big news for slaves in the paper and brought it back for me to read. The war was over and the slaves were free. They continued to get the paper and have me read it to them. One day I saw your mother's ad. I divided up everything of value."

She leaned her head on his shoulder and sighed. "I don't want you to think I sat in the cook house. I worked the fields, the garden. I cooked and chopped wood. I defended what was mine and I buried many men."

Parker put his arms around her, and that made her feel safe. That life in Tennessee was gone now. Her heart didn't feel so heavy anymore. He laid them down and he cradled her to him. Even though he didn't love her, he cared.

CHAPTER TEN

*P*arker eased out of bed, went down to his study, and paced back and forth for most of the night. She'd been through more than he could have possibly imagined. Since she'd been a virgin, he thought she'd been spared the worst part of war for women. Oh, but what a woman she was. She had risked her life to help everyone on the plantation. Most women would have searched for an available man to take care of them but not his Georgie. She was one of a kind.

What was the key to her heart? She'd allowed and even enjoyed limited intimacy while they traveled in the wagon. Then everything had gone downhill. She'd been so strong for so long and when they married, he'd told her she was safe but she hadn't been. She'd been treated worse by his mother and Taggart then any soldier could have.

Didn't she realize that when he said he loved her he had meant it? He stopped in mid-step. When was the last time he'd told her? Blast it! He hardly ever told her. No wonder she had left without leaving a note. He planned to court her, but he never got around to it. He'd have to do better. They could have a loving marriage if he could get all the misunderstandings cleared up. Apparently, the greatest one of those was that he didn't love her.

She still didn't like being touched, but it wasn't from the overseer's assault on her; it was from the whippings she survived in this very house. He'd take every opportunity to touch her as he could. She'd get used to him, wouldn't she?

What if the whole problem was she didn't, couldn't love him? He started pacing again. She loved him once; he'd have to try for a second chance. He was a clueless fool. He left her in bed alone too much.

He went to their room and took off his clothes. He stared down at her face, lit only by moonlight coming in the window. She looked so serene, untainted by the world. She was beautiful, but for some reason she didn't seem to realize it.

He slipped under the covers and spooned Georgie pulling her as close as possible. She was so soft and warm against him and now holding her he couldn't imagine being upset with her. She stirred and he kissed her temple, rubbing his cheek against her soft hair until she sighed and snuggled against her pillow.

It was torture to just hold her when he desired her so much, but he got a hold of himself and eventually fell asleep.

She was still in his arms when he woke the next morning. As soon as he opened his eyes, he could see that she was awake. He tightened his embrace, and she placed one hand on his arm.

"This feels nice." She turned in his arms and stared into his eyes. "I don't want any more bad feelings between us. I know you don't have it in you to love me, but we can try to make the best of it, don't you think?"

Before he could refute her assertion that he couldn't love her, she was out of bed, and his ability to speak failed him. He'd tell her the truth later in the day. Right now, the view was too incredible to interrupt. He did wince when looking at the scars on her back. But he hadn't known Taggart had it in him to be so evil. If he ever caught up to him...

"Eggs or pancakes?" She smiled shyly.

He grinned at her. "I have to say your pancakes are heavenly."

"Pancakes, then. I'll get busy. See you downstairs."

He'd have given anything to have been able to pull her back into bed. Patience, he'd need to dig deep to gather all of his patience. He hoped he had enough. But she was wrong about him not having it in him to love. He loved her enough for both of them.

He hurried and got dressed and shaved. He planned to kiss her and wanted his face to be smooth. He was nervous and he almost laughed at himself. She made him feel young and unjaded.

After he made it downstairs, he stood in the kitchen doorway just watching her at the cook stove. In three long strides, he was behind her. He wrapped his arms around her waist and kissed her neck, behind her ear, and finally her cheek. "Those smell good."

"I don't think you'll like them burned," she teased.

Her lighthearted voice made his heart soar. "If it means I get to hold you like this all morning I wouldn't care if they were charred on both sides."

Her laugh was melodious, and he let her go. "I'm not sure what's gotten into you this morning but go pour yourself a cup of coffee and sit down." She shook her head at him while her smile widened.

"If you insist." He did as she said and then sat at the table. "Did you know your hips sway in a very womanly way when you move? It's hard for me to concentrate when I watch."

She quickly turned around. She shook the spatula at him. "You are no gentleman, Mr. Eastman."

He chuckled. "I never claimed to be, Mrs. Eastman." He waited until she put all the food on the table before he pulled her down onto his lap. "You are the prettiest filly I ever did see."

She turned her head to meet his gaze. "Filly? I'm hoping that's some type of Texas compliment." Her eyes were filled with humor.

He thought his heart might burst, looking at her. "It's a compliment of the highest order. I do wonder why you shy away from compliments, though."

"Compliments were always meant for my sister, never for me, and I guess I just don't know how to receive them. Parker, I do know how to view myself in a mirror, and I already know I'm plain to look at. It's fine, really. I've been told so all of my life, and I've accepted it as fact."

He turned her so she sat sideways almost facing him. Cupping the sides of her face, he pulled her in for a kiss. He started with a light, slow kiss, and when he heard her little groan, he claimed her lips as his own. He deepened the kiss, and his heart pounded painfully against his ribs when she wrapped her arms around his neck.

Pulling away, he was touched at the dazed look in her eyes. "I have a few things I need to get done, but I'll be home early. Maybe we could go riding together." Her answering smile was all he needed.

"I thought you'd never ask. I've been feeling better for days." She stood. "Do you want more coffee?"

He got out of the chair and encircled her with his arms then kissed her cheek. "No, the sooner I head out, the sooner we can go for a ride."

Georgie spent a big portion of her day sewing. She turned a full brown skirt into a divided skirt for riding. Sewing was easier when she wanted to do it. Plus it was really altering the skirt, not creating one from scratch. Putting it on, she was amazed that the length of both sides of the skirt were just about the same.

Confidence that had once deserted her now filled her. She had to take back what was hers. She was a survivor and could do whatever was necessary to stay alive. She'd allowed Taggart and Millicent to steal it from her. Taking it back felt wonderful, and somehow gave her a sensation of having power. She need not doubt herself.

Most of what happened had been out of her control. Parker's too for that matter. They were stronger together than apart. And besides all that, he was a good kisser. He was good at other things too. Her face heated as she thought of their intimacy, which had led to the creation of their child. They could try again.

He was showing her a lot of affection. A brave move considering he had no real way of telling how she'd react. Hopefully, he'd be home soon. Spending time together could only help. Her heart fluttered; he really thought her pretty.

She was pulling on her brown leather boots when Parker walked in. His smile lit the whole house. He didn't seem to be as nervous as she.

"Are you ready, Mrs. Eastman?"

"I'm all yours, Mr. Eastman." She blushed when he cocked his right brow.

"The horses are saddled. I thought we'd ride to the highest point on the ranch. The view is amazing." He took her hand, entwined his fingers with hers, and led her outside.

The sun seemed brighter than ever, and the grass greener. It must be due to the joy in her heart. For a moment, her natural urge to guard her heart and withdraw was strong but she fought herself and won. She wanted to experience happiness even if it didn't last.

When they reached the barn, Parker separated his hand from hers. He stepped inside and came back out with his arm behind his back. "I have something for you." He grinned and brought forth a bouquet of sunflowers. "These are for you."

She took the flowers and stared at them.

"Is something wrong?" he asked his voice full of doubt.

"Oh, no. It's just that I've never received flowers before. I'm…stunned." She touched the soft yellow petals. "Thank you so much." She hugged the flowers to her chest. He made her feel like a young girl again. "I never realized just how wonderful it is to receive flowers from a man. My sister would have known how to bat her eyelashes, smile, and say thank you. I'm a bit backward in the man department."

She took a step toward him and tugged on his shirt until he was low enough for her to kiss. How much of a kiss was appropriate? Perhaps a quick one would do. As she started to let him back up, he put his arms around her, pulled her to him so their bodies touched, and deepened the kiss.

When he was done, she stood there and stared at him. "I, um, I…I think I'll put these in water. I'll be right back. She raced to the house. He must think her dim witted. She hurried and put them in a can filled with water and practically walked on air back out of the house.

Parker had led the horses to the front porch. Before she even had a chance to think, he placed his big hands on her waist and lifted her up. Her divided shirt was perfect. It was already a great day. After making certain she was settled in the saddle, he mounted Mine and off they went.

The rode in a direction she'd never gone before, and the area was beautiful with clear water creeks, live oak trees and plenty of open land. The climb was gradual and it was a wonder when they arrived at the top. Parker jumped down and was by her side in an instant. His grin was as wide as the whole outdoors, and she eagerly went into his embrace. He held on to her for a moment then took her hand.

"This way."

They didn't walk far before they stopped and she swore she could see all of Texas. The sky was so blue, and a lake shimmered in the distance. A lot of cattle dotted the hills. Several groves of trees had been planted in straight rows.

"What type of trees are they?"

"Those are pecan trees. My father planted them the same year we moved here. We take the pecans to the general store, and Anson sells them for me. We ate a lot of pecans the year I got back."

"It's spectacular, Parker. Where does your land end?"

He chuckled. "All you see is ours. That's why when I go and check on the land it can take a few days, depending on what is going on."

"Now I understand. Thank you for bringing me here. I enjoy spending time with you. Parker, I want to make a real go of our marriage. Will you be able to put Rose Callen behind you? I know she hurt you something terrible, but—"

Parker took her into his arms and kissed her. "Rose is my past, love. You are my future." He reached into his pocket and he pulled out a ring. "I know I have more courting to do, but I love you and I don't want there to be any doubt." He knelt on one knee and held out his hand. In his palm a slender circle of gold glinted in the sunshine. "Georgie will you do the honor of wearing this wedding ring?"

Tears filled her eyes. "Yes, Parker, yes." She could feel his love as he put the ring on her finger and gazed at her. After he stood, she threw herself into his arms. "I love you too, Parker. And I want children, lots of children."

"There's only one way I know to get you with child." Parker grinned as her face heated. Then he kissed the side of her neck and froze in place, staring beyond her toward some bushes. He automatically pushed her down to the ground and drew his gun.

Fear coursed through her as she followed his gaze and spied the Confederate uniform. Why hadn't she brought her gun? There was no movement, but she was still frightened as Parker walked closer.

He turned and frowned. "I know where Taggart is now. He's mostly buried."

"How did he die?"

"I don't know, and I don't care. I'll have someone move him to a deeper grave away from this spot." Parker helped her off and dusted her off. "You're trembling."

"Old fears I guess. He forever marked me with his whip, and I hate to say this, but I'm glad he's dead."

He held her tight. "I confess I'm glad too. I really don't care who killed him. More than likely it was one of my soldiers. They don't condone mistreatment of women."

She lay against him with her ear over his heart, and the steady beat calmed her. "Let's not let him ruin our day. I like when you court me. Or has that come to an end now because I'm wearing your ring?"

"Georgie, I do believe the best is yet to come."

EPILOGUE

*G*eorgie sat on a blanket under a tree. The cooler weather had been a godsend for her. She still didn't feel all that well in the mornings. Whenever she sat, she instinctively put her hand over her stomach. Which would it be; a boy or a girl? Parker just kept saying as long as the baby was healthy. Men! Couldn't they make up their minds? She wanted a little boy; one to carry on his daddy's name and who would grow to help Parker on the ranch.

She glanced around at all the happy faces. It was Founders' Day, and she had talked Parker into having the festivities on his land. No one wanted it near town and the soldiers. Even the store owner, Anson Stack, was there along with Shelly Kingsman. They had both closed their businesses for the day.

What amazed Georgie the most was the amount of people who came. She didn't think so many people lived in Spring Water. Parker had been right when he told her most people avoided the town. Everyone she met had been so very nice with a few exceptions. Fanny Chancellor was one. She was still a snob and had dressed in high fashion for the day, but wearing a hooped dress to the picnic hadn't been such a good idea. Georgie had forgotten just how careful one had to be wearing such a contraption. Sitting was uncomfortable, one tended to hit others with the hoop when walking, and the list went on. Fanny still stared at Parker with yearning. Well, too bad.

The other was Rose Callen. Georgie actually felt sorry for her. The man she'd married instead of Parker had left her as soon as she became pregnant, and after the baby was born, she had returned to Spring Water in disgrace. Rose had the saddest eyes, Georgie had ever seen. Her son was almost one year old and a handful. Rose looked at Parker with such longing in her eyes and the whole town had turned their backs on her.

Whoosh, Rose's son had fallen into Georgie. Georgie laughed and hugged the boy, talking to him until he calmed. Rose hurried over, her eyes filled with fear.

"Rose, please sit and keep me company. Your son is adorable. What's his name?"

Rose's jaw dropped, but she sat down. "Henry, his name is Henry. If I stay and talk to you the rest of the town won't like it." Her voice cracked.

"Nonsense. I don't care what they have to say. It must be hard caring for a son alone. I only say that because Parker and I will be having a child soon enough. Would it be presumptuous if I sent over a basket of food every now and then? I firmly believe that women should help other women. We don't have many employment opportunities and there are some men who take advantage."

Rose looked down at the blanket, not saying a word.

"Rose, you must be a sweet woman for Parker to have once loved you. I want to help you, and I'd like to be your friend. As you can see no one else is sitting on my blanket talking to me."

"I can't take charity."

"Rose, put your pride aside for your son's sake. I'll come up with some type of plan for you where you can be with Henry without having to be at the mercy of any man. The war left so many women defenseless, and it's not right. Please say yes."

"Now what's this boy's name?" Parker asked as he picked the child up.

"That is Rose's son Henry. Isn't he darling? I was just telling Rose that we want to help her. It's too hard to be a mother alone."

Rose stood up. "I don't want to be a bother, Parker."

Parker smiled. "Rose, take the help. Henry here has more energy than all three of us together. I wish no ill will. Plus, once Georgie gets an idea, I find it easier to just step aside and let her do it."

"Thank you, both of you. I will take some help. The Union Soldiers have been…"

"That's the end of that. Good riddance, I say."

Rose took Henry from Parker. "Thank you again." She hurried off.

Parker sat down and put his arm around Georgie. "You have a kind and generous heart."

Tears filled her eyes. "She's wearing rags, and she is so thin. Henry could use more food too. She made a foolish choice, but I reaped the benefits. She'll be just fine."

"Are those going to be just a few tears or are we going to water the whole prairie?"

"I see your lips twitching, Parker Eastman. It's just a few tears. Did you win at shooting?"

"No, Walter outshot me."

"Too bad I couldn't participate. I would have won." She chuckled.

"So you think it's funny do you?" Parker kissed her neck until her face flamed.

"You wait until I get you home!"

Parker grinned. "What did you have in mind?" He leaned over and kissed her tenderly. "We'd have the house to ourselves."

"Let's go! Have I told you I love you?" She stroked his cheek.

"Yes let's go, and I'll show you just how much I love you." He stood and helped her up.

Georgie stared out at the crowd with her hand over her unborn child. There had been so many times when she'd thought her and Parker would have to part. But the love in her heart now told her that everything she needed was right here with this special man at her side. Finally their tattered hearts had become whole.

THE END

I'm so pleased you chose to read Tattered Hearts, and it's my sincere hope that you enjoyed the story. I would appreciate if you'd consider posting a review. This can help an author tremendously in obtaining a readership. My many thanks. ~ Kathleen

ABOUT THE AUTHOR

Sexy Cowboys and the Women Who Love Them...
Finalist in the 2012 and 2015 RONE Awards.
Top Pick, Five Star Series from the Romance Review.
Kathleen Ball writes contemporary and historical western romance with great emotion and
memorable characters. Her books are award winners and have appeared on best sellers lists including: Amazon's Best Seller's List, All Romance Ebooks, Bookstrand, Desert Breeze Publishing and Secret Cravings Publishing Best Sellers list. She is the recipient of eight Editor's Choice Awards, and The Readers' Choice Award for Ryelee's Cowboy.
Winner of the Lear diamond award Best Historical Novel-Cinders' Bride
There's something about a cowboy

facebook.com/kathleenballwesternromance

twitter.com/kballauthor

instagram.com/author_kathleenball

So Many Roads to Choose

The Settlers

Greg

Juan

Scarlett

Mail Order Brides of Spring Water

Tattered Hearts

The Greatest Gift

Love So Deep

Luke's Fate

Whispered Love

Love Before Midnight

I'm Forever Yours

Finn's Fortune

52662118R00105

Made in the USA
Columbia, SC
05 March 2019